Chasing Perfect

VICTORIA JAX

CRANTHORPE
—— MILLNER ——
PUBLISHERS

First published by Cranthorpe Millner Publishers (2025)

ISBN 978-1-80378-307-9 (Paperback)

www.cranthorpemillner.com

Cranthorpe Millner Publishers

Printed and bound by CPI Group (UK) Ltd
Croydon, CR0 4YY

MIX
Paper | Supporting
responsible forestry
FSC® C013604

To the best life partner
anyone could ask for

Chapter 1
Sienna

"So, how was the birthday sex?" Chloe asks, shimmying her shoulders as Amber sits down across from me.

Amber huffs and shakes her head. "I didn't get any." Her cherry-coke hair gleams in the sunlight streaming through the cafe windows, and her blue eyes stand out against her pale skin. "We were just about to, and then... 'Mommy, my tummy hurts!'" she mock-whines. "There's no bigger turnoff than a puking child."

I shake my head, taking a sip of my iced mocha, the cold spreading through my hands as I cradle the cup. "That really sucks."

"That's what I get for not finding a sitter."

"Did he at least get you a present?" Chloe asks, leaning forward with interest.

"Well..." A hint of a smile tugs at Amber's lips. "When I got home from work, he had put *all* the laundry away. And he got me this necklace."

She lifts a silver heart necklace, the light catching the polished surface. The metal has been twisted to spell out 'MOM'.

"Oh wow," Chloe gasps.

I can't tell if her enthusiasm is as fake as mine is about to be or if her response is genuine. The necklace is obviously something her boyfriend picked up at a gas station from the Mother's Day section. Oh, sorry, *and* he did a chore. Give the guy a fucking medal.

"It's pretty," I tell Amber, forcing a smile. "Does he always combine your birthday and Mother's Day?"

Amber shrugs like it's not a big deal. "Yeah, ever since the boys were born."

I struggle to mask my disappointment. My friend deserves so much more.

"Is Anthony watching the boys now?" Chloe asks.

"Yeah. He usually has his mom over to help."

"It's only for a couple hours," I say, my voice firm. "He can't watch them by himself?"

"The boys are a handful right now," Amber explains, a hint of defensiveness in her tone.

I give her a pointed look. "If you can do it, so can he."

She leans back in her chair and looks away.

End of conversation, I guess. Amber never did like me criticizing her bare minimum boyfriend, but I can't help it. My girls deserve better than a man whose idea of a gift is doing the laundry.

"Chloe, how are you and Ben?" I ask, steering the conversation towards something less contentious.

"It's not really 'me and Ben'," she says. "He still doesn't want to be exclusive."

"How long have you been sleeping together now?" Amber asks.

"A few months," she tells Amber, feigning indifference. "It's not a big deal."

I open my mouth to say something, but Chloe cuts me off.

"V, you've been awfully quiet."

Veronica, the brunette to my right, has been avoiding our gazes all morning, her fingers tracing the rim of her coffee cup.

"What's going on?" I prod gently. "Is it Marcus?"

V has been talking to Marcus for weeks. She was smitten, but he made his intentions clear from the start. He'd practically begged her to let him into her bed, but she refused unless he took her on a date first—as she should, in my opinion. My heart breaks for her as I take in the sadness on her face, and we all reach for her as tears well up in her eyes. Her delicate frame brings out a protective instinct in all of us.

"I gave in," she whispers.

"Oh, honey," Amber comforts her, squeezing her hand.

"I haven't heard from him since," V continues dejectedly, a tear slipping down her cheek.

"Let's get some pastries to make you feel better."

Amber rises and heads to the counter, her movements swift and purposeful. She's always been the mom of the group, making sure we take care of ourselves. I worry that her caring instinct is why her boyfriend seems to get away with doing so little.

I focus on comforting V. Her situation reminds me of my own past, dark memories resurfacing. Memories I've never shared, not even with my closest friends.

Amber returns before I can bring myself to voice my thoughts aloud, and we eat in awkward silence until she breaks the tension with a soft giggle.

"I'm sorry, I just... how did he not break you in half?"

I look at Amber in horrified disbelief, but V bursts out laughing, joined swiftly by Chloe. What the hell? V was pressured into sex, and my friends are *laughing* about it?

"Oh, lighten up," Chloe says, elbowing me in the side. "V's fine, aren't you, hon?"

V smiles, squeezing my hand reassuringly. "I'm okay—it was all consensual. I'm just upset that he ditched me afterward. Honestly, I've been more stressed about telling you all. I thought you'd be disappointed in me for not holding my ground."

"Oh, honey, of course we're not disappointed," Amber chimes in, wrapping her arms around V again.

"Don't be dumb, V. I'm surprised you held out as long as you did," Chloe reassures her. "He might be an asshole, but Marcus was hot. Besides, not everyone takes sex as seriously as Sienna."

I cross my arms over my chest. "Maybe you should. Then you might have a boyfriend who respects you," I retort.

"At least I'm getting some regularly, Ms. Three Year Dry Spell," she snaps back.

Chloe and I have always clashed. Honestly, I think she's still bitter that my hair stayed blonde while hers turned brown in middle school.

She takes a drink of her water. "I'm just saying, if you lowered your standards, you'd have a man in your life, too."

I cross my arms, biting my tongue to keep from saying I'd rather die alone than settle for a man who only wanted me for my body. I could try to convince them that they need to respect themselves by demanding respect from the men in their lives, but it wouldn't make a difference.

I uncross my arms and relax my posture. "I just wish you guys saw yourselves the way I see you."

4

"Aw, tear," Amber says as she drags a finger down her face, quoting *Bring It On*.

The nostalgia brings a soft smile to my face. I might not always understand their choices, but I love my girls. I'm grateful the squad has stayed together.

"Now come on," Amber continues, "we've all discussed our love lives except you, Sienna."

"There's nothing to tell." I shrug.

"You haven't been on any dates?"

"A few. None of them impressed me."

"Did any of them make it to a second date?" Chloe asks, exasperated.

"Nah," I reply, sipping my coffee. "I mean, come on. If I ask about your hobbies, then you ask me about mine. It's not that hard."

Amber rolls her eyes. "You don't even give guys a chance."

"They're the ones that need to impress me. It's like I always say—"

"*The egg don't chase the sperm!*" they chant in unison.

"Well, it doesn't!"

Chapter 2
Sienna

Amber and I stroll down the bustling sidewalk, our footsteps in sync. The squad has been together since middle school, but Amber and I go back to elementary.

She's normally the talkative social butterfly of the group, always lifting everyone's spirits with her lighthearted stories and jokes, but I can tell something is off with her today. The usual sparkle in her eye is missing, replaced by something akin to anger.

"Did you start that book I got you for your birthday?" I ask gently, trying to draw her out.

"Yeah," she murmurs, still avoiding my gaze.

I stop walking and turn to face her, placing a reassuring hand on her arm. "Okay. What's going on? You usually love talking about books."

She shrugs and continues towards the gym, forcing me to jog along after her. The usual energy between us feels muted, and I need to get to the bottom of it.

"Does this have something to do with you not getting a coffee this morning? You didn't eat anything either."

She looks away, confirming my suspicion without saying a word.

"Amber, you have to eat." I take a protein bar from my bag and offer it to her.

She takes it gratefully. "You have no idea how hard it is to look good after you've popped out two kids," she confesses, her voice tinged with frustration and a touch of sadness.

I grab her arm, looking into her dark blue eyes, willing her to believe me. "Listen to me. You are beautiful. You are gorgeous. You are stunning." My words are sincere, and I hope they break through her self-doubt.

She gives me a weak smile. "Thanks, but we can't all be Sienna Machlan, can we?" she remarks bitterly as she pushes open the doors to the gym.

Her words sting, but I know they're not meant to hurt me—they're born from her own insecurities.

It's not my fault that my job keeps me in shape. Working as a Pilates instructor at three different gyms makes it easy to sculpt my body. It's hard sometimes, sure, but balancing workouts with motherhood must be a thousand times harder. I don't know how she finds the time to exercise at all.

As we make our way through the lobby, a couple of gym bros turn to watch us walk by.

"See?" Amber murmurs to me. "I'm not the one turning all these guys' heads."

"Who cares about impressing guys? We're doing this for ourselves," I remind her as we link arms and head to the studio for the ten o'clock class. Part of my job is to encourage women to work out as an act of self-love, not to achieve external validation.

"Of course, of course." Her tone brightens. "You're still on the market, though. I'm sure you could have any guy in here." She looks around, scanning the gym. "Anyone catch your eye?"

I look around too, but the gym is mostly empty, except for

a few early risers.

"Nah," I reply with a shrug.

I give Amber's arm a reassuring squeeze as I silently vow to be there for her and show her just how strong she is.

"Great job, everyone," I yell to my class of sweaty, tired women as they trickle out of the room, their faces flushed with exertion but glowing with satisfaction.

It was a tough class, but they all powered through. That's what it's all about, I think to myself, smiling with pride.

I lock the door to the studio on my way out, waving goodbye to Amber before she heads back home. Her wave is half-hearted, her earlier mood still lingering. As I watch her disappear down the hall, I make a mental note to check in on her later. I should check in on V, too.

To keep my muscles loose, I walk around the track on the upper floor until my next class. Coffee with the girls this morning was a weird one, and I can't stop thinking about Chloe's snide comment.

I make a loop around before I text Chloe and apologize for my comment this morning. My friends are important to me, and if she wants to sleep with a man who doesn't want a relationship, that's her choice.

Sometimes I forget that not everyone was raised with the same values I was. My mother taught me to never chase butterflies—they will simply fly away. Focus on building your garden, and the butterflies will come to you. She instilled in me pride, confidence, and the importance of demanding respect, especially from men. Those lessons have shaped me, for better or worse.

I'm lost in thought, looking down at my phone, when a man jogs up beside me.

"Hey there," he flirts, his voice carrying a hint of playfulness.

I shamelessly look him up and down, taking in his blond hair and broad shoulders. "Hi," I reply with a smile, intrigued by his bold approach.

"Would you like some company?"

Cute *and* polite? I'll take it.

"Sure," I say as he falls into step next to me. "I'm Sienna."

"Jake," he replies, maintaining a respectful distance. "You teach Pilates, right?"

"Yep, that's me."

His eyes light up with interest. "I'd love to take your course. It's a women's only class, though."

"Actually, it isn't. Anyone can sign up. But a lot of the moves are too hard for men," I tease. "It requires a certain balance and flexibility that men just don't have," I say, purposefully challenging him.

"I seriously doubt that's the reason there aren't any men in there. I'm sure I could handle it."

"Care to put your money where your mouth is?" I flirt back, feeling the thrill of competition.

His grin widens. "Bring it on."

We step off the track and find two yoga mats, laying them side by side. The gym is still relatively quiet, with faint sounds of weights clinking and music in the background. I instruct him to lie on his back, mirroring my position on the adjacent mat.

"Lift your legs to a forty-five-degree angle," I instruct, demonstrating the position.

He's clearly struggling already, and I can't hide my smile.

"Now lift your head and shoulders and extend your arms straight in front of you."

He copies me, smirking as if he accomplished something.

"Now we scissor-switch our legs. Like this." I demonstrate by moving opposite legs, one over the other, my movements fluid and controlled.

He manages two switches before dropping his head and legs onto the mat.

"How the hell do you do that?" he grunts, watching me continue with ease.

"I guess there are some things a woman's body can do that a man's can't," I tease, resting on the mat and enjoying my small victory.

"Why don't you come back to my place, and I'll show you what a man's body can do."

Taken aback by his sudden change in tone, I sit upright, flustered. "Oh, I..."

"I'm sorry," he interjects, sitting up as well. "I thought you were flirting with me."

"No, I was," I explain quickly, trying to salvage the conversation. "I don't know you that well. I mean, we just met."

"Oh, you're one of *those* girls," he says, disappointed.

"Excuse me?" I reply, my brows furrowing.

"You know, the kind that makes a guy wait three dates," he says dismissively.

I cross my arms, not bothering to hide my frustration and

disbelief. "It's not about the number of dates."

"Well I'm not gonna keep buying you dinner just for a chance to sleep with you," he says, his voice dripping with irritation.

I roll my eyes. "I didn't realize you were one of *those* guys," I retort, throwing his words back at him.

He stands up to leave, leaving me sitting on the mat as he walks away. "Fucking tease," he mutters under his breath.

At least he showed his true colors early on. He probably got intimidated by a woman outperforming him. I'm just glad I didn't waste any more time on him.

Hugging my knees to my chest, I let the weight of the encounter sink in. Clearly I'm attracting the wrong kind of butterflies.

Chapter 3
Liam

The waitress pours coffee into my mug before moving to the other side of the table to fill my mother's.

"Happy Mother's Day," she says with a practiced smile. "You must be the mom of these two fine young men."

"Yes, I am," Mom says proudly.

"I can see where they get their good looks from." The young woman's eyes drift not-so-subtly over my brother and me, and I struggle to hold back a cringe. "I'll give you some time to look over the menu," she says before walking away.

After we look over our menus, Mom turns to Nathan.

"I feel like it's been forever since you've been home. What's new with you?"

"Oh, not much. College. You know how it is."

Nathan's the rowdy one of the two of us, always drawing attention to himself, not that he doesn't live for that.

"Studying hard, I hope?"

"Oh, absolutely," he answers cockily.

Everything he does, he does cockily.

Mom rolls her eyes affectionately. She knows all about his partying. "And how's Riley?"

"She's great. She landed that internship for the summer."

"Oh, that's wonderful!"

Mom's always been supportive of Riley's aspirations to be

a lawyer. I admire her drive, though she could definitely do better than my brother. Still, at least the chances of Nathan completely fucking up his life are a lot slimmer as long as he's tied down to someone like her.

The waitress returns to take our orders. She ends with me, and I tell her, "I'll have the steak and eggs. Steak medium and eggs over easy."

"Good choice. I can tell you have good taste," she says, winking at me, her eyes lingering longer than necessary.

I keep my expression deadpan, not wanting to give her the wrong impression. I'm spoken for.

The waitress's flirtatious behavior doesn't go unnoticed by my mother, who smiles in amusement.

"Damn, you don't need to be rude," Nathan interjects after the waitress leaves, breaking the silence with his trademark bluntness.

"I'm taken."

He shrugs. "No harm in playing the field. You may want to keep your options open."

I know he's just teasing, but it pisses me off when he makes light of my relationship just because we haven't been together for as long as him and Riley.

"I have a girlfriend."

"Yeah, but it's nothing serious," he replies, shrugging off my relationship status as if it were inconsequential.

"Actually, it is," I snap, failing to mask the anger in my voice. "I'm going to propose."

He's visibly taken aback, his usual bravado faltering. I can't help but feel a twinge of satisfaction at catching him off guard.

"Oh, honey, that's wonderful!" Mom exclaims, her eyes

sparkling with genuine happiness at the prospect of another addition to the family.

I knew she would be excited. She adores Anna and sees her as the perfect daughter-in-law.

"I haven't bought a ring yet, but I want to." There's not an ounce of hesitancy in my voice despite the magnitude of the decision I'm about to make.

"You've only been together six months," Nathan says. "Don't you think that's a little soon?"

I shrug. "We both want to get married one day. Why wait?"

He looks at me knowingly, waggling his eyebrows suggestively. "Oh, I know exactly why you're in a hurry to marry her."

"It's not like that," I say sternly. I don't appreciate the insinuation. "She's interviewing for a job this weekend. It's three hours away, and I need to show her I'm serious about her. If she gets the job, I'm going to move there with her."

Sadness overtakes my mother's face. Her initial excitement fades with the realization that our family dynamic might change soon. I hate disappointing her, but Anna is the one. I'd follow her anywhere, and Mom knows that better than anyone.

My phone vibrates in my pocket, and I pull it out to see Anna's name on the screen.

I smile as I answer. "Hey, baby. How'd the interview go?"

I spy Nathan out of the corner of my eye, mocking me with exaggerated gestures and mouthing '*hey, baby.*' I choose to ignore his antics and focus on Anna's voice on the other end of the line.

"Fine," she answers. "I got the job."

She doesn't sound excited, so I wait for her to continue.

"Liam... listen," she starts hesitantly. "I'm taking the job here. I'm not coming back."

My face drops, and Mom and Nathan awkwardly avert their gazes. "What do you mean?"

"There's nothing there for me," she says quietly.

My world stops spinning as her words repeat in my mind. *Nothing*.

I'm nothing to her.

"What about me?" The desperation in my voice is painful, even to my own ears. My stomach churns as I realize what's happening. "I'll come with you."

"I don't want you to. I'm sorry, Liam."

She hangs up.

I slowly lower my phone from my ear, only now noticing the food in front of me. Fuck, even the waitress heard me get dumped.

We sit in uncomfortable silence until Nathan, predictably, cracks a joke.

"Want me to get the waitress's number for you?"

I glare at him, but he just shrugs. I'm not surprised. He doesn't take anything seriously.

"Not the time, Nathan," Mom scolds. She reaches across the table and takes my hand, her eyes full of sympathy. "I'm so sorry, sweetheart."

The sheer embarrassment of the situation makes me want to crawl into a hole.

I sit there miserably as I try to process everything. The steak and eggs sit untouched in front of me, suddenly unappetizing. I thought things were going great. I thought she felt the same way.

Mom looks at me with pity, and I want to disappear from this restaurant. "Sometimes people change their minds. It doesn't mean there's anything wrong with you."

"Yeah, it just means she's an idiot," Nathan adds.

My patience with him has worn thin, but I know he's just trying to help in his own way.

Mom pats my hand. "Why don't we try to enjoy the rest of our breakfast?"

I nod, trying to muster some semblance of normalcy. We eat in awkward silence, but I've lost my appetite.

"Well, if you ever need a wingman, you know where to find me," Nathan says between bites. "Are you gonna finish that?"

I roll my eyes and push my plate towards him.

Chapter 4
Liam

It's been two weeks since Anna left me.

It's pathetic how much I'm moping about because of her.

How could she do this? I was willing to do anything for her, even move three hours away. I would have left my friends, my family, even my farm for this woman. That's how special she was to me. But apparently, I meant nothing to her.

Nathan has been on me to move on for the past week. He's tried to set me up twice now with some college girls he knows, but I can't bring myself to meet them. I refuse to waste my time on someone who won't be loyal to me.

I'm not asking for much. I just want someone who will be as committed to me as I am to her. Loyalty is everything to me, and Anna betrayed that. Even if she came crawling back to me, I wouldn't take her back.

I sit on the couch in the dark of my starter house. I haven't put much effort into making it a home; I'll inherit my dad's farm in less than a year, and I plan on selling this place and moving out there. I'll be able to work from home and set my own hours rather than having to go into the office every day.

I stare at the ceiling, listening to yet another playlist I made. Some would call it depressing. I call it... Yeah, it's depressing. But it's the only thing that seems to soothe the ache in my chest, even just for a moment.

A knock on the door interrupts my thoughts, and I have a feeling I know who it is. I reluctantly rise to answer it, bracing myself for the inevitable intrusion into my solitude.

"Pack your shit, let's go!" Nathan barges in, followed by his girlfriend, Riley.

I have nothing against them showing up here unannounced. I just prefer to deal with my emotions alone.

"I told you, I'm not going. I'd like to be left alone."

"Dude, it's Memorial Day weekend. Are you seriously not coming to the lake house?"

"I'm seriously not going," I say, leaning back against the countertop with my arms crossed.

"But it's tradition! We play cards, smoke stogies, and drink whiskey by night and beer on the boat by day. It'll be fuuuun," he singsongs. His attempt at persuasion falls flat against my stubborn resolve to remain in my misery—alone.

"I'm not in the mood to have fun."

"You never are."

"Cut him some slack, Nathan. It's only been two weeks," Riley cuts in. I appreciate her attempt at mediating the tension, something she has to do fairly often when it comes to Nathan and me. Riley loves partying as much as Nathan does, but while they have many of the same vices, she keeps him grounded. In other words, she's his perfect match.

Nathan shrugs. "So?" he says dismissively. His cavalier attitude only serves to fuel my irritation. "They weren't even together that long."

"Get out." I've reached my breaking point with his insensitivity. "I told you I'm not going, so leave."

"Fine, whatever."

With a frustrated huff, Nathan storms out, Riley trailing behind him after sending me an apologetic glance.

I lock the door behind them, the sound of their departure marking the return of my solitude.

Collapsing onto the couch, I turn the music up even louder.

It doesn't matter how long we were together: Anna was the one that got away. And I'll spend forever wondering what I did wrong.

Chapter 5
Sienna

My feet are killing me. I swear I'm getting blisters from these too-tight heels.

As we walk—well, hobble in my case—my date drapes his jacket over my shoulders, a point in his favor. But considering that I can't even remember his name, we won't be going on a second date.

It doesn't help that neither of us can think of anything to say; we've exhausted all topics of conversation at dinner. The bustling sounds of the city streets provide the backdrop to our awkward stroll back to my apartment.

The pain in my feet forces me to slow down, and he matches my pace. When he mentioned he didn't have a car, I debated whether it was even worth going out with him. Then I reasoned it wasn't fair to judge him since I don't have a car either.

As it turns out, lack of transportation is the only thing we have in common.

He offers his arm, and I take it gratefully. "I borrowed these shoes from a friend," I explain to justify my hobbling. "They're a bit small."

"It's not too much further to your apartment."

His response does nothing to reassure me, but I appreciate the gesture, trying to quicken my pace. Hopefully V won't mind a bit of blood in her shoes. The image of her shaking her head at me when I return them brings a smile to my lips, a fleeting moment of humor during an otherwise lackluster evening.

Once we finally reach my apartment building, he follows me up the metal stairs. We stand in front of my door, the harsh lights above forcing me to squint as I look up at him.

My date—Greg? Craig?—kisses me on the cheek.

"Can I see you again?" he asks hopefully.

"I'll think about it."

I return his jacket, and he walks away, disappearing into the night without a second glance.

As soon as he's out of sight, I unlock the door and step inside, closing it behind me before slumping against the wood. There was nothing *wrong* with my date. He complimented my dress, asked all the right questions, and paid for dinner. There was just no spark.

Once again, I consider Chloe's words from our coffee meet-up: if I lowered my standards, I would have a man in my life. She's probably with Ben right now, warm in his bed, 'getting some', as she would put it. Meanwhile, I'm alone in a cold apartment on a Friday night with no romantic prospects in sight.

I look around my studio apartment. I've tried to make it feel like home—plants, pictures, wall lights—but it just doesn't. The tight space triggers my claustrophobia. I can't wait to move somewhere far from the city... if I ever have the *funds* to move anywhere, let alone buy property.

Removing my heels, I rub my aching feet. A shower is tempting, but I decide against it, opting for silk pajamas and fluffy pink slippers. I pour a glass of strawberry lemonade and coconut rum, then plop down on the couch to unwind.

I sit in silence, wishing I at least had a dog to keep me company. I'd love to adopt one, but an apartment in the city is no life for a dog.

Halfway through my drink, I decide it's time to seriously rethink my life. I must be doing something wrong. I need to take control, decide what I want, and make it happen.

Grabbing a notebook and pen from the coffee table, I make a list of everything I want in a partner.

The words flow from my pen with a sense of purpose.

Handsome
Respectable
Has a good job
Mature
Owns land or wants to own land
Respects me and my choices
Likes my friends

I survey the list with a sense of satisfaction. There *must* be guys out there who meet these criteria. I'm not asking for a billionaire.

I finish my drink and decide that I will not continue seeing a man unless he checks all of these boxes. This list serves as a promise to myself, a commitment to prioritizing my own happiness. I deserve nothing less than a partner who can fulfill my basic requirements.

I lean back on the couch, proud of myself for figuring out what I want. The list was step one.

Now it's time to make it happen.

Grabbing my laptop, I set it on my lap, its screen casting a cool glow in the dimly lit room. My thoughts are hazy from the long day and alcohol, but I refuse to let that stop me from embarking on my quest for a partner.

I start with LinkedIn. My man's gotta have a respectable job, after all. Sure, my mother taught me to be independent, and I am. But as a Pilates instructor, there's a limit to how much money I can earn. I've embraced my career, but I can't do it forever, and the prospect of greater financial freedom and the ability to indulge in life's luxuries beckons me. I want to be able to afford the finer things in life, maybe go on vacation once in a while. Most importantly, I've got to get out of this soul-sucking apartment.

With LinkedIn open in incognito mode, I search for 'employees' near me. The screen before me shows a digital dating pool, presenting me with an abundance of options. Each profile is a potential suitor, each job title a glimpse into their world. As I scroll down the page, I take in the array of men and women, weighing their professions against my criteria. It feels like perusing an all-you-can-eat buffet. With each click, I compile a selection of suitable prospects.

Once I have about twenty tabs open of attractive men near me with respectable jobs, I decide to widen my search by fifty miles. If I want to get out of the city, I need to consider guys who don't live here.

Expanding my radius, I jump into a digital sea of potential matches, scrolling past countless profiles.

I scroll and scroll and scroll—until I find him.

Liam Wright.

Something about his picture draws me in.

I click on his profile, eager to learn more. On his page, I see the picture a bit bigger. He's not standing in front of a blank wall or in an office; he's standing in front of a field that goes on for miles. His baseball cap hides dark brown hair, and his jeans and boots give him a rugged look. He stands confidently and smiles at the camera.

I pretend for a second that he's smiling at me.

Chestnut brown eyes seem to gaze into my soul, and I close my eyes and imagine that short, thick beard bristling against my face as he kisses me.

Shaking myself out of the fantasy, I read his professional profile. He graduated college the same year as I did, got hired right away by a big company, and has been a software engineer for three years.

I happily close the tabs of other contenders, my focus now solely on Liam, and open a new one to look up 'software engineer salary'. What comes up has me dropping my jaw. $250,000 a year. Clearly I got into the wrong profession.

Liam seems to fit my criteria pretty perfectly so far. I close my laptop and unlock my phone to type his name into Instagram. I find him quickly, and his profile picture ignites something inside me. He sits on a tractor with tires as tall as me, biceps flexing as he maneuvers the machine. The tires on it are as tall as me, and I'm pretty sure I've never seen anything sexier.

Realizing I should probably make sure it's not the alcohol talking, I make my way to the bathroom for a long, hot shower. As the water cascades over me and sobers me up, I become more confident about my decision to reach out. This could be the beginning of something extraordinary—a chance to break free from the confines of apartment life and meet someone I actually have a chance of a future with. I hop out of the shower and towel off.

Pulling on my white silk pajama set, I lie on my bed with my phone in hand, ready to immerse myself in Liam's digital presence. With each image and post, I uncover facets of his personality that resonate with mine. He doesn't post much, but every picture convinces me I've made the right choice. He's ruggedly handsome, outdoorsy, and probably doesn't have a girlfriend since there are no pictures of him with a woman.

I stop to think for a moment. Should I do this? There's nothing wrong with reaching out to someone I want to get to know. And it's not like I only want him for his money—that's just a bonus. His picture is what caught my attention and stirred something inside me I thought was dormant. And maybe he's looking for a girlfriend.

I take a deep breath. I'm hesitant to abandon my entire philosophy by making the first move. What would the squad say? But I'm tired of this apartment. I'm tired of getting the bare minimum from guys. I'm tired of sleeping alone.

Am I really going to do this?

I scroll to another picture. A border collie licks his face while he laughs.

Yes.

Yes I am.

Chapter 6
Liam

A loud ding jolts me awake, and I open my eyes to see the ceiling lit up by my phone screen. It's probably a text from Nathan, saying something along the lines of 'dude, you should be here!'; 'dude, come up here'; 'dude, I just jumped the fire pit, it was awesome'. I don't have the energy for his ridiculous escapades tonight.

My phone screen goes dark, and I roll over to go back to sleep.

After a while, I give up, reluctantly checking my phone in case it's something important.

It's not a text, and it's not from Nathan. It's a DM. From someone I don't recognize.

Wide awake now, I turn on the bedside lamp and unlock my phone. Sitting back against the headboard, I read the message.

Sienna.M.14

Hey there, I never do this, but I really like your profile picture. I'm Sienna.

It's probably just a bot or a scam, but I decide to open up her profile anyway. The first picture shows her in a tight black dress that shows off her toned body. She stands in a bedroom with her hands fluffing up her honey-blonde hair in a carefree, purposefully sexy way.

I'll admit, I'm intrigued. If this girl is real, she's incredibly attractive.

No harm in responding, just in case.

Wright24

Hey there, I'm Liam. Thanks for the message. I like your profile picture too. Tell me a little about yourself.

I scroll through her other pictures. She's effortlessly pretty, with wavy golden hair and warm hazel eyes. She takes a lot of photos with friends, but she's the one that stands out. I keep scrolling down her page, and each picture gives me a glimpse into her life. Whether she's in a nice dress, athletic wear, or a cozy sweatshirt, she looks stunning. Her life seems filled with laughter and good times, her carefree spirit shining through, drawing me in.

Sienna.M.14

Hm, let's see. I'm 25, currently working as a Pilates instructor, teaching three times a day. Outside of work, I mostly hang out with friends or go on nature walks, but I live in the city, so I don't get to do that very often. What about you?

I keep scrolling through her pictures until I get so far down that I'm looking at her old cheerleading photos. Feeling like a perv, I scroll back up. It's clear she has a zest for life, and I wonder if we might actually hit it off.

Wright24

Sounds like you have a good work-life balance.
I'm a software engineer, so I spend a lot of time
at work. I like to hunt and fish on the weekends,
though, and I like to cook when I can, more than just
the deer I shoot and the fish I catch lol.

I wait for her next message, but it doesn't come right away. Maybe she fell asleep. Maybe she changed her mind about me. More time passes, and I wonder if I said the wrong thing. Did I come on too strong? Or maybe too boring? My mind races with possibilities.

Sienna.M.14

I have to admit, I like a guy with a rugged lifestyle.
Here in the city, it's mostly pretty boys and posers.

I exhale in relief that she answered, though I'm not sure why. There's something genuine about her messages that makes me want to believe she's not just a scammer. I'm still skeptical that I'm actually talking to a pretty girl, but if Sienna *is* real, I'd be stupid to throw away this opportunity.

Wright24

I'd love to show you around the countryside if that's
something you'd be interested in.

Again, she doesn't respond right away. I sit there in the dark, waiting for another message from her. After five long minutes, I start to worry I went too far or misread things.

Finally, she responds.

Sienna.M.14
I'd love that! As long as you don't have a girlfriend or anything. Do you want to meet for coffee tomorrow morning?

As I read her message, I realize I haven't thought about Anna once since Sienna messaged me. Maybe this is what I need, a fresh start with someone new.

As I answer her message, anticipation for our date tomorrow sends a thrill through my veins, something I haven't felt in a long time.

Chapter 7
Liam

Sitting alone at a table, I watch the door expectantly. I arrived early out of habit, and I've been sitting here reevaluating my life choices ever since. It's way too soon to be dating again. I'm not even close to getting over Anna. My heart still aches when I think about her, and I wonder if this 'date' is just a desperate attempt to fill the void she left behind. Not to mention that Sienna, if she is real, is not my type. Like, at all.

I need a girl who's down to earth. Practical and rational. Maybe I've got her all wrong, but she seems like the type to throw caution to the wind. She's sexy and fun, but she's not long-term girlfriend material. Maybe I should just leave.

Then again, what's the harm? I should at least give her a chance. I've been feeling sorry for myself for too long, and a selfish part of me can't wait to see the look on my brother's face when he sees Sienna on my arm. I might as well have as much fun with Sienna as I can. I'm probably just a new thrill for her; she'll decide she's had enough of me eventually.

I'll just have to try not to get too attached.

The chime above the door catches my attention, and I glance over.

There she is.

Sienna.

Golden hair lit up by the sun streaming through the glass,

tan skin standing out against a blue and white sundress. I track my gaze down her smooth, tan legs to her heeled sandals. She's gorgeous. And, more importantly, real.

A man walks in behind her, so close that he's almost touching her. She smiles when she sees me, then turns to talk to him. Okay, I guess she knows him. Why would she bring another guy to our coffee date? Do I have this totally wrong? My mind races with doubts and questions, and something else that feels almost like jealousy.

The man stays by the door as she starts to walk towards me. Oh, right. She's meeting a stranger from the internet. He's here in case this isn't a coffee date. Guilt instantly squirms in my stomach as I realize I was worried about feeling like a fool while she's been worrying about potentially being kidnapped or worse.

Humbled, I stand up as she reaches my table, and she hugs me as if she's known me for years. I stiffen instantly, not used to such casual affection, but her hold doesn't loosen, and the tightness in my muscles eases a fraction as her scent envelops me. She smells sweet and delectable, like coconuts and something else.

She pulls away before I can place it, and I find myself wanting to be closer to her to smell it again.

"Should we get coffee—"

"I like your boots—"

We talk at the same time.

"Thanks—"

"Yeah—"

We speak at the same time again. Giggling, she takes my arm, and we head to the barista at the register. If this is how often she's going to keep touching me, I'm not sure I'll get through this date without combusting.

"Medium black coffee, please."

"The usual for me," Sienna says beside me.

The barista rings up a double chocolate mocha with extra whipped cream, and I try not to shake my head.

Once I pay for it, we walk to the pick-up counter.

Sienna looks up at me through her lashes as we wait. "You're so tall," she says with a smile.

Even with her heels, she barely comes up to my shoulder. I don't know how to respond, so I stand there awkwardly. She gives a subtle thumbs-up to her bodyguard at the door, and he walks out.

"Friend of yours?" I ask.

"He's my brother's friend."

I nod, mostly because I don't know what else to do.

The barista hands us our coffees, and I grab a single sugar packet before we return to our table.

"Only one?"

"I like to actually taste the coffee," I tease, glancing at her chocolate milkshake.

Once I finish stirring, I look up to see Sienna smiling.

She sits tall and proud, and her eyes gaze deep into mine. "I'll try yours if you try mine," she offers.

She doesn't seem to be feeling awkward at all. In fact, she's perfectly at ease being on a first date with me. I can't decide whether her confidence is intimidating or inspiring.

"Okay," I tell her, sliding my coffee over. "You first."

She picks it up carefully and brings it to her lips. Her full, soft, shiny lips. I can't tear my gaze away as she takes a delicate sip. She grimaces at the taste, and it's fucking adorable.

"It's..." She sets it back down. "... very flavorful."

I can't help but chuckle.

Instead of annoyance, she meets my amusement with a grin, pushing her own drink towards me. "Okay, now you go," she says excitedly. I give her a quick glance before I put the straw between my lips. The taste is too sweet on my tongue, especially first thing in the morning.

"That is chocolate milk," I say matter-of-factly.

She bursts out laughing like I'm a fucking comedian, and some of the nervous tension between my shoulders melts away. Her laughter is contagious, and my lips tilt up a fraction. Maybe this date won't be so bad after all.

Chapter 8
Liam

I still can't believe she's real. Not only that, but she's actually interested in me. She's made that clear with her coy smiles, intense eye contact, and fascination with everything I say. Her eyes sparkle every time I speak, and I feel a rush of excitement every time she smiles at me.

The initial awkwardness has faded some as we've talked, but her flirting is a little overwhelming. I'm not used to this much attention. My brother is the one who draws attention to himself; he's the wild card, the show-off. And that's fine by me. I like being on the sidelines.

"I'm surprised you work with computers if you like working with your hands," Sienna comments, glancing at my hands wrapped around my coffee cup.

"It's not so bad," I tell her. "That's where the money is. I figured it would be a reliable job."

As I talk about my job, I realize how practical I sound, but it's true. I've always wanted stability; it was something Anna admired about me. My mind drifts to her like it has every day for the past two weeks. From what I've gathered, Sienna is Anna's polar opposite, but maybe that's what I need right now.

Sienna slowly brushes her hair off her neck, tossing silky golden waves over her shoulder. "That's very mature."

I barely register what she says as I take in her smooth, tan, flawless skin. Her low-cut, strappy sundress shows off her shoulders and chest, and a dainty gold chain with a teardrop-shaped diamond adds to her elegance. Her effortless grace captivates me, and I find myself staring for a bit too long.

I lean back in my chair, subconsciously spreading my legs and putting my arm around the empty chair next to me. It's a territorial gesture, some evolutionary response to being in the presence of a beautiful woman.

"So," she begins, "Tell me about your family."

"Well..." A drop of her sugary coffee drink spills over the side of her cup. "It's just my brother and me..." She slowly slides her finger up the side, collecting the droplet. "My parents live in..." I lose my train of thought as she lifts her finger to her mouth and sucks on the pad. I clear my throat. "... Lakeshore," I blurt out. "What about you?"

She talks cheerfully about her family in her angelic voice, and I try to pay attention. I really do. But the way she's playing with her necklace draws my attention to her cleavage. Although I suspect that's on purpose.

An image pops into my head of her lowering the straps of her dress and letting it fall to the floor. She stands in front of me in her underwear, perfect skin just begging for my touch. I picture her toned body straddling mine as she wraps her arms around my neck.

"... and then I moved here," she finishes.

I clear my throat again, forcing my mind out of the fantasy, and nod as if I actually heard a thing she said.

My heart races as I think about what just happened. No one has ever had this effect on me. I'm always level-headed and grounded.

As if she can read my thoughts, she gracefully slides into the chair to my right so that my arm is around her and our knees touch slightly. The proximity makes my stomach flip, and I breathe in her coconut and vanilla scent. Her closeness is intoxicating, and I feel my resolve slipping.

Having this seductive woman by my side has me feeling cocky, and suddenly, I want everyone in this cafe to know she's with me. I glance around, half hoping someone I know will walk in and see me with her. It's a childish thought, but I can't help it.

She leans into me and glances at my lips, then back up to my eyes. I consider kissing her—clearly that's what she wants—but I can't. I barely know this girl. Yes, she's sexy as hell, and I'd love to take her home with me, but that's not the kind of guy I am. I jerk my arm back and cross both in front of me. I want to get to know her better before we do anything.

She takes the hint and sits up straight in her chair. "So, tell me about your farm," she says, dipping back into our conversation as though nothing happened.

"Well, it's not really my farm. It's my dad's."

I tell her about the land and what we do there. How my brother and I grew up spending the weekends there. For some reason, I leave out that I'm going to inherit it when I turn twenty-five. I've already shared more than I usually do.

As I talk, her eyes light up more and more. I can't tell if she's genuinely excited or just pretending. Either way, her attentiveness makes me want to keep talking to her about anything and everything.

I find myself opening up more than I have in a long time,

and it feels surprisingly good to get back out there and meet someone new. Sienna might be the perfect woman to bring me out of my funk. She knows exactly the effect she's having on me—she must do—but none of her behavior feels forced; everything about her screams genuine.

Sitting here with her, talking to her... it ignites something inside me, knocking me off-kilter and making me question myself.

It's terrifying and exhilarating all at once.

Chapter 9
Sienna

I have no idea if this is working.

I can always tell when a guy is interested—he flirts back, he touches me, he smiles—but Liam's stoic demeanor is throwing me off my game, making me second-guess everything I do. Even my best moves have had no effect: drawing attention to my chest and shoulders, sucking a drop of coffee off my finger, even the Marilyn Monroe triangle method. My flirting *always* elicits some reaction, but with Liam, there's nothing.

It's frustrating, yet oddly intriguing.

I thought he might have been flirting when he spread his legs out into a cowboy pose, taking up more space and showing dominance the way men do—a classic signal I've seen countless times. But when I moved closer and leaned in, he drew back from me. Maybe he's just not the type to respond to overt advances. The last thing I want to do is make him uncomfortable.

I decide to scale back the flirting and just keep it casual.

"I've talked enough about myself," he says in that low, sexy voice of his. "How did you get into Pilates?"

"I just took a course and loved it. My instructor was awesome, and she made me fall in love with challenging my body, so now I motivate other women to challenge their bodies. I teach at three gyms, so I have a pretty wide audience now."

He nods in understanding. His intense gaze makes me feel like I'm revealing more than just career details.

"Why so many gyms?"

"The one I spend the most time at pays me the least, so I have to make up the money elsewhere." I shrug. "But it's fine. It keeps my body in shape doing it so often."

"Why don't you quit the gym that pays you the least? Then you'd have more time to teach at a gym that pays better, or you could do something else."

His practical suggestion makes sense, but it's not that simple.

"You make a good point, but I can't quit. It's a small gym, and my course brings in a lot of money for the owner."

He wraps his large hands around his coffee cup, a concerned expression on his face. "Are you sure the owner's not taking advantage of you?"

His protectiveness makes my heart flutter in my chest... though I suppose he might be like that with everyone.

"She wouldn't do that. She's the best. We've become friends over the past couple of years."

He frowns. "If it's not financially viable for you to continue working there, I really think you should consider quitting. It's not fair on you to be working for less than your teaching is worth."

His persistence is surprising, and it makes me wonder why he cares so much.

"I can't. I'm too loyal. She took a chance on me when I was fresh out of college. Hired me with no experience. Plus, she needs me. I can't just abandon her—"

The intensity of his stare stops me mid-sentence. Clearly something I said struck a chord. His deep brown eyes seem to gaze straight into my soul, unnerving me. Does he think I'm being foolish by wasting my time at a small gym when I could be making more money doing something else? Or does he admire my willingness to support my friends? He's impossible to read, and I finally tear my gaze away, feeling uneasy.

He reaches for my hand, instantly drawing my focus. God, his hands are so warm, smooth with calloused fingertips. I look up and meet his gaze, relieved to see a flicker of warmth in his eyes.

"I think that's really cool," he finally says.

I breathe a sigh of relief, and my nerves melt away. Me, nervous around a guy? That's a first.

"I'm going to be honest," he tells me, his voice lower than before, "I was hesitant to meet you today. But I'm really glad I did."

"I'm glad you did, too. Just out of curiosity, why were you hesitant?"

He seems to think it over. "You're not anything like the girls I usually date."

"Are we taking a trip down Ex-Girlfriend Lane?"

"I'd rather not," he says with a chuckle. His laugh is so sexy. "I just mean I usually go for more... outdoorsy women. Someone who'd rather go fishing than shopping for purses."

I sit up straight in my chair. "I'm offended you think I can't do both."

"I didn't say you can't," he defends himself. "I'm just saying, I highly doubt you fish." He glances pointedly down at my manicured nails.

"Actually I do," I lie, partly because I want to be his type and partly because I want to prove him wrong.

He shakes his head, his lips tilting up at the corners. I decide then and there that making him smile is my new goal.

"Alright then. Let's go fishing."

"Can't wait."

Chapter 10
Sienna

When I return to my apartment, I dive into an afternoon marathon of fishing tutorials. How did girls get a boyfriend before the internet?

I watch countless videos on how to bait a hook, how to cast a line, how to gut a fish. I can't let on that I've never fished a day in my life—I have to at least *look* like I know what I'm doing.

The intricacies of fishing, which I had always dismissed as simple, are actually ridiculously complicated. I take notes, replay the videos at half speed, and practice the motions in my living room, feeling both determined and nervous.

Once I've seen practically every fishing tutorial on the internet, I decide I'm ready. Now that I know the basics, it can't be that hard. I'm actually kind of excited to fish with Liam. And the thought of spending the day with him, no matter what we do, sends a thrill through me.

I smile to myself. He wants to see me again. He's picking me up tomorrow to take me to his parents' farm, and we're going to spend the entire day on the dock by the pond, just the two of us. His family is out of town for the weekend, so we'll have the whole property to ourselves.

I close my laptop and head to my bedroom, taking in my appearance in the full-length mirror. I'm pretty sure Liam's not into the whole dressed-up city-girl look, which is fine by me. I'd be more than happy to never wear stilettos again. Still, I want to look desirable. Hot, but not too showy. I can do that.

I start by pulling off my bracelets and rings, then I unfasten my necklace, returning them to my jewelry box. I remove my press-on nails next—I won't be able to bait a hook if my nails are long. The sound of each nail being peeled off feels oddly symbolic, like shedding a layer of my old self.

Digging through my drawers, I pull out a comfortable pair of blue cotton shorts and set them on the dresser. I pair them with a white V-neck tank top that will show off some stomach. Staring at the simple outfit, I feel oddly giddy at the thought of impressing Liam, showing him a whole new side of me.

Grabbing my backpack, I fill it with snacks, bug spray, sunscreen, and a sweatshirt for the evening before retrieving my hiking boots from the back of my closet. It's been too long since I've worn them, and I can't wait to get them dirty again.

With my clothes picked out and a new education on fishing, I lie on the bed, anticipation buzzing in my veins as I wonder what tomorrow will bring.

I wait by the door for Liam to text me he's here, and I'm surprised when he texts and asks for my apartment number.

A minute later, a knock echoes through my small apartment. I open it to see Liam standing there, dressed in his signature jeans and boots with a black t-shirt and ball cap—his presence filling the doorway. None of my dates in the past two years have actually come to the door to pick me up for a date.

His old-fashioned manners bring a smile to my face.

Not wanting him to see how small my place is, I step out and quickly close the door behind me. As I lock up, I ask Liam for the farm's address. He's skeptical about why I need to know, but he gives it to me anyway. I decide not to mention that it's for the 'in case something happens to me' text I'm about to send Amber.

As we descend the steps, excitement bubbles inside me, mingled with a hint of nerves. I really want to show him I can get my hands dirty—figuratively, of course. I still plan to follow my five-date rule, no matter how attractive and gentlemanly he is.

"You look nice," he says, breaking the silence with his low, throaty voice.

"Thanks. So do you."

I follow him to the far side of the parking lot, where a lifted black truck towers over the other vehicles. It's more practical than flashy, but still sexy as hell.

"This is me," he says, gesturing to the truck with a hint of pride.

"Of course you drive a truck," I tease, hoping for a smile.

He keeps his face stoic as usual, but he surprises me by opening the passenger door for me. His chivalry makes my heart flutter. I try to remember the last time a guy gave me butterflies.

It's been a while.

Sure, some of the guys I've dated have opened the odd door for me, but none of them have been as consistently and effortlessly chivalrous as Liam.

Hopping up into the truck, I put my bag in the back seat as

he walks around and gets in the driver's side.

Liam turns the key in the ignition and puts his arm behind my headrest, backing out of the spot with ease. I can't take my eyes off him, the way his large hand grips the steering wheel. I'd love to feel that hand on my thigh, the heat of his skin against mine.

Wearing a ball cap and sunglasses, he somehow looks both ruggedly handsome and adorable. He doesn't seem to notice me staring, or he doesn't care, so I continue to watch him as we ride in silence. Usually, I'd try to fill the quiet with chatter, but the silence between us feels strangely comfortable.

Once we hit the highway, I turn to face him. "Do you always wear a hat?"

"Yes."

"Do you always wear *that* hat?"

"No."

His curt responses make me smile. I consider it a challenge to draw more out of him.

I sigh and face forward again, taking in the scenery.

Another ten minutes pass, and the city gives way to a patchwork of fields and forests.

"Can *I* wear your hat?"

He doesn't answer, and just when I think he's going to ignore my question, he surprises me.

"As long as you treat it like a cowboy hat."

My brow furrows. "What does that mean?"

"Take the cowboy's hat, take the cowboy home."

My jaw drops at such a crude statement coming from his mouth, and my cheeks heat with the implication. He glances at me with a sly smile, his lips curling into a slight grin that sends a chill through me.

I can't help but laugh. "I like that."

I smile to myself as I look out my window. I must be doing something right. Not only is he taking me to his family's farm, but I also got him to flirt with me.

Chapter 11
Liam

Sienna's eyes go wide as I pull into the long driveway. She looks left and right as she takes everything in, a huge smile lighting up her face. I'm still skeptical that anything will come out of this trip, but her excitement is infectious, much like her flirting.

I can't believe I was so bold in the car ride over.

Gravel crunches under the tires as we approach the old but sturdy farmhouse my father bought back when he was my age. I come up here every other weekend to take care of the place, but I have to admit, it gets lonely.

For a moment, I imagine being greeted by a pretty smile and a warm embrace, the sweet scent of coconut enveloping me.

I need to get a grip. Seeing Sienna's enthusiasm for my soon-to-be home is overtaking my rational mind.

As soon as I park, she jumps out of the truck, throwing her arms out and spinning. "There's so much space out here!" she yells, her voice echoing in the open air.

Her blonde hair fans around her as she spins, and her carefree elation shines through.

I grab her bag from the back and head toward the front door. "Kinda hard to have a farm without space," I say sarcastically. I unlock the door while Sienna looks around with childlike enthusiasm. She's so goddamn adorable I have to force myself not to stare at her like a creep.

She follows me through the front door and kicks off her boots, her eyes darting around eagerly. "Show me around!"

Setting her bag down on the table, I gesture toward the kitchen. "There's the kitchen." I turn and gesture again. "There's the living room, and there's the bathroom."

When I turn back around, she's already halfway up the stairs. "Is your room up here?" she calls down.

"Yes," I reply, following her. I open the door to my childhood bedroom and lean against the doorway as she steps inside like she owns the place, her eyes scanning every corner.

The small room holds only a bed and a dresser. Some of my old stuff remains, but it's underwhelming, to say the least.

"I bet you have lots of memories in this house," she says, smiling softly at me.

Her warm gaze entrances me, and for a moment, I'm lost in those hazel eyes.

"Yeah," I answer, nodding and looking around.

She's looking up at me like she expects something from me, but I have no idea what, so I turn and head back downstairs.

She follows me down the steps to the back door. When I slide the curtains open to reveal the backyard, she gasps.

I unlock the sliding door, and we step onto the back porch. The large covered porch holds two porch swings and a set of tables and chairs, but the view is what's truly breathtaking. The yard encompasses three acres of grass, with a playground, a tire swing, and a small garden. Beyond the yard, trees stretch as far as the eye can see.

Sienna's face lights up with wonder, and she slips off her socks to run through the grass barefoot. I shake my head, amused by her childlike energy. I've never met someone who is so unabashedly themselves. She moves with such grace and freedom. Like she belongs here.

A quiet voice inside me suggests that maybe she does.

I follow after her to the tire swing, and she hops onto it and throws her head back, her laughter filling the open space. Giving the tire swing a push, I step aside to let her swing by. She laughs uninhibitedly, and the beautiful sound stirs something in my chest. I could get used to having her here.

I shake my head as I watch her laugh and spin. I can't even remember the last time I played in this backyard. It feels like a lifetime ago.

When she finally slows down, I take her hand to help her out of the swing. She holds onto it for balance, and her hand feels tiny in my own. The softness in her touch makes my heart race.

She looks up at me with shining eyes. "Do you want a turn?"

"No," I say, shaking my head at the ridiculous notion of her pushing me on a tire swing. "I'm good."

I guide her up the porch steps, and we sit on one of the porch swings. With my hand still in hers, she rests her head on my shoulder. We look out at the backyard.

Feeling her body so close to mine only stirs up more of the strange feelings that have been plaguing me since I picked her up this morning. I can't help but imagine us both living here a year from now. It'd be nice to have company, someone to sleep next to every night and wake up to in the morning.

I'm being ridiculous. I just met her yesterday. It seems like every girl I start seeing, I see a future with. I need to cool it with

Sienna and take it slow.

The swing rocks gently back and forth as the sun moves across the sky. Despite the perfect weather here on my farm—my happy place—and the beautiful woman beside me, sadness finds me. It was supposed to be Anna here with me. We were supposed to get married and move in together. I can't believe I was ready to propose. She would've said no if I had asked. At least she saved me from that embarrassment by breaking things off before I had the chance.

Sienna tilts her head to look into my eyes. She smells heavenly, and the sunlight illuminating her golden hair gives her an angel-like glow. She seems to sense my sorrow because she gives me a soft smile.

"Do you want to go fishing now?"

Chapter 12
Liam

Sienna leans back on her elbows and lets her bare feet dangle over the edge of the dock. She's completely at home here, and I wonder if she feels that way everywhere or if this place is special. Or maybe it's me she's comfortable with.

The thought gives me a primal sense of satisfaction.

She's a vision next to me with her flawless tan skin and barely-there clothes, but I keep my eyes forward, her long legs and white toenails in my peripheral. She has her pole set up next to her while I hold onto mine. I was surprised when she actually baited her hook on her own. Her delicate fingers deftly handled the task with a skill I didn't expect from a city girl.

We've been sitting here in silence for almost twenty minutes. If she's waiting for me to talk, she shouldn't hold her breath. I quite enjoy the silence. I find immense pleasure in the tranquility of the pond and the gentle lapping of water against the dock.

She looks over at me smugly. "I told you I can fish."

I chuckle. Her smug expression is adorable, and my pride swells that she's comfortable enough to tease me. "You proved me wrong."

Another ten minutes go by of us sitting in companionable silence, nothing but the sounds of nature around us: birds chirping, the occasional splash of fish jumping, and the rustling of leaves in the breeze.

"So, did you and your brother fish here together growing up?" Sienna asks, breaking the silence.

"Sometimes."

She simply nods and takes a drink from her cup, content with my brief response. I appreciate that she doesn't press for more.

A tug on my line brings my attention back to the pond, and I start reeling it in. Sienna sits up with bright eyes, excited to see what I pull in. I yank my pole back and reveal a bluegill about ten inches long. Sienna scoots away quickly, then composes herself.

I scoop the fish into the net and remove the hook from its mouth. Out of the corner of my eye, I notice that Sienna has moved two feet further from me, her reaction a mix of horror and fascination.

Once I remove the hook, I hold the bluegill in my hands and face her. She's horrified by it but forces a smile.

"Nice job," she rushes out, looking back and forth between me and the flopping fish in my hands.

A smirk forms on my face. "Come look at it."

She shakes her head. "I can see it from here."

I hold it closer to her, and she stands to back away. I stand up and walk closer until she's leaning against the railing.

I can't help but laugh. "You don't fish, do you?"

"No," she admits. "Make it stop looking at me with its fishy eyeball!"

"What, this?" I joke as I lift it higher.

She squeals and leans back further into the railing, causing it to break and sending her falling backward. I reach out to catch her, releasing the fish back into the water, but she grabs my shirt and pulls me down with her, plunging us both into the icy pond.

I spit out murky water as I come up for air and touch the top of my head, my hat lost somewhere in the water.

The shockingly cold water invigorates me, but I don't know how Sienna will react. She'll probably demand I take her home, slap me in the face, or... laugh?

She's laughing.

Waves of relief wash through me, and I laugh along with her. I haven't had this much fun in a long time.

She swims closer and wraps her arms around my neck, her wet hair clinging to her face, droplets of water sparkling on her skin in the sunlight. Without thinking, I place my hand on her back, our noses almost touching as our chests rise and fall, her soaking wet body pressed against mine.

Breathing heavily, I gaze into her eyes, and she tilts her head slightly. I tilt mine the other way, preparing for our lips to touch.

I turn my head at the last second.

"I can't do this." The words come out softly, regretfully.

The confusion and hurt in her eyes breaks my heart.

She pulls back slightly, her expression shifting into understanding.

"It's not that I don't want to," I begin, struggling to find the right words. "It's just..."

"You don't have to explain."

Chapter 13
Sienna

Liam takes my hand and helps me out of the pond. Dirty pond water drips from our bodies onto the grass, and I look down to discover that my white tank top is see-through.

Good.

I want Liam to notice, to kiss me like he was about to before he stopped himself.

"Sorry about that," Liam says, stoic as always. "The dock is pretty old."

"It's fine. I'm the one who broke it."

"It was falling apart anyway, don't worry," he insists. He jogs back onto the dock to grab our stuff.

Once he returns, he hands me my bag and boots, just now noticing my shirt.

Being the perfect gentleman he is, he looks away politely.

Damnit.

"I have some clothes you can change into."

"That'd be great. Thanks," I say awkwardly. Not because of the shirt, but because of the almost-kiss we should probably discuss.

The tension between us mounts as we head back to the house, walking on the winding path through the trees. The forest is alive with the sounds of birds and other animals, and I decide to break the silence between us. "Sorry your fish got away."

Liam simply glances at me and continues walking. "I'm the one who should apologize."

"It's not your fault the railing broke."

"About what happened in the water." Liam sighs, running his fingers through his hair, now bare of the cap he lost in the pond.

We make it to the clearing behind the house and walk through the backyard.

"I, um... I just got out of a relationship... two weeks ago."

"It's only been two weeks?" I ask softly.

He nods, and the pain in his eyes makes me want to wrap him up in a big hug. God, I feel like such an idiot. I've been flirting incessantly with him, coaxing him into flirting back, and he's only just broken up with someone else. Someone important, by the look on his face.

We walk up the back porch steps, and I stop him before he can open the door.

"Liam, I understand if—"

"I want to keep seeing you," he interrupts, his voice gentle but firm, determined.

My eyes widen. Maybe I haven't messed this up after all.

I smile at him, feeling uncharacteristically shy. "I'd like that."

He slides the door open, and we leave our boots outside. "Come with me," he says, guiding me through the house to the stairs. His hand rests on my lower back, warm against my cool, wet shirt, and despite having just met him yesterday, I feel safe with him.

Once we reach the upstairs bathroom, Liam turns on the

shower. "I'll be right back with a towel and some clothes."

I use the time alone to take in my reflection. In the artificial light of the bathroom, I can see my lacy white bralette through my see-through white tee, and I wonder if my appearance got Liam flustered. His emotions are buried deep—I'll have to learn his tells—but he certainly seemed attracted to me in the water. The thought of him feeling desire, or maybe even arousal, sends a thrill through me. Guys lusting after me is nothing new, but something about Liam tells me he's not like those guys.

I take a moment to inspect my face, relieved that I went light on the makeup today, otherwise I'd look like a raccoon. My hair is in a far sorrier state, though. Before I can run my fingers through it, Liam returns and sets the clothes and a towel on the sink.

"Thanks," I tell him as he starts to leave, hoping he'll take a quick peek at my see-through top.

No such luck.

Sighing in defeat, I remove my clothes and step under the stream of the shower. The freezing cold pond was a touch beyond refreshing—it's not quite swimming weather yet. As the hot water thaws my icy skin, I can't keep the smile off my face. The fishing part of our date was a disaster, but Liam *likes* me. He almost kissed me, and he wants to keep seeing me.

I want to squeal and do a little happy dance. I know I have to be patient—he's only just broken up with someone, after all—but I have a feeling it will be worth it.

Lathering myself in his body wash, I contemplate the sadness on his face earlier on the back porch. I wonder how serious their relationship was. I want to ask him, but I'm not sure if that's the best way to get him to open up. There's so much I want to know, but I don't want to push him so soon.

After rinsing off, I step out of the shower and towel off. I look through the clothes he's placed beside the sink: an old shirt of his and some plaid pajama pants. I'm tempted to step out naked just to get a reaction from him, but I reign myself in.

My bra and underwear are soaked with murky pond water, so I leave those hanging on the shower rod and pull his shirt and pants on. I feel a little weird not wearing underwear with someone else's pants, but there's not a lot I can do to fix that.

I smile at the sight of myself in his clothes as I attempt to finger-comb my hair. The smell of him on the shirt he lent me oddly comforts me, like he's giving me a constant hug.

Heading downstairs, I find Liam sitting in the living room, freshly showered and changed. The blankets, board games, and crayon drawings hung on the walls give the place a cozy, lived-in vibe.

He looks up as I enter, his eyes softening when he sees me.

I settle into the seat beside him, our knees touching. I know he might not be ready to kiss me, but I can't stop myself from trying to maintain some kind of physical connection.

"Thanks for the clothes."

He simply nods, his gaze distant. "Do you want to stay for a while?"

"Sure, if that's alright."

"Of course."

Tentatively, I reach out and gently rub his back, feeling the tension in his muscles.

He turns to look at me with a pained expression. "Be patient with me," he says quietly, his vulnerability catching me off guard.

My heart melts, and I want to wrap a blanket around his shoulders and kiss his nose. I settle for giving him a soft smile and a kiss on the cheek. He leans into my touch, and the world outside fades away.

"How about a movie?" I suggest, wanting to keep our afternoon going.

"Sure."

I stand and turn out the overhead light, switching on a lamp before I open the drawer of movies.

I dig through the DVDs and discover they cater to a different audience—namely, preteen boys. Titles like *Transformers*, *Scooby Doo*, *Jurassic Park*, *Spider-Man*, and so on.

I decide on *Scooby Doo*—an old childhood favorite—and join Liam back on the couch.

The movie starts, and I snuggle close to Liam under a blanket. He wraps his arm around me, and we sit comfortably as the movie plays.

It's nice to watch something mindless. Life's always so busy when I'm working, and even on weekends I'm always going out with the girls or on dates. It's relaxing to just coexist in the same space with someone without the constant pressure to make conversation.

The movie ends an hour later, and we head into the kitchen.

"Can I make you dinner?" Liam asks.

"I'd like that."

"How does pizza sound?"

"It sounds awesome," I reply, opening the freezer. "There's no pizza in here."

"I said I was going to *make* you dinner," he clarifies, pulling out flour and olive oil from the pantry.

After washing his hands, he combines the two ingredients, adding yeast, water, and salt to the mixture.

I hop up onto the counter and watch his large hands knead the dough with practiced ease. Carefully, he flattens it out into a circle on the pizza pan before opening a can of tomato sauce and pouring it into a saucepan. He adds garlic, olive oil, oregano, and other ingredients and stirs the mixture with purpose. I wonder to myself whether my friends' boyfriends have ever put this much effort into a dinner, if they even know how to cook.

I'm mesmerized, watching him intently as he lifts the wooden spoon to his lips for a taste.

"Do you want a taste?" he asks.

I nod eagerly, and he leans towards me, lifting the spoon to my mouth. I don't detect any hint of a suggestive tone, but then it is Liam... I can never get a read on him when it comes to flirting.

I take a small taste, the rich flavors spreading across my tongue. "That's really good."

A hint of a smile tugs at his lips. "Can you grab the cheese?" he asks, returning his focus to the saucepan on the stove.

"From the fridge, or do I have to go milk a cow?"

He lets out a chuckle. "No, it's in the fridge. The cows aren't mine. I rent the space to ranchers."

Pleased with myself for making him laugh, I hop off the counter and open the fridge, spotting a block of mozzarella in a drawer. I grab it along with two bottles of beer.

"I thought this was your parents' farm?" I inquire, handing him a beer.

"I'll inherit it next year."

"Seriously!" I close the space between us and hug him from behind, my enthusiasm deflating slightly as he stiffens.

No surprise affection—I'll need to remember that.

"This will all be yours?" I press, my arms loosening slightly but remaining around his waist.

He nods stiffly, and I let him go.

"So, are you gonna live here?"

"Yup."

For someone about to inherit and move into a beautiful farmhouse in the middle of the countryside, he doesn't sound all that happy. He continues cooking in silence, spreading the sauce over the dough before grabbing a grater and shredding the cheese over the pizza.

As he works, I try to come up with reasons why he would be sad about inheriting acres of farmland. I can't think of any as he puts the pizza in the oven and starts the timer.

"Do you not want to live here?" I eventually ask.

"It's not that. I love this place. I just thought things would be different."

We move to the table and sit next to each other.

"How do you mean?"

He takes a deep breath, like he's psyching himself up to speak. "I wanted to propose," he admits, his voice heavy.

I instinctively place a hand on his back.

"She broke up with me on the phone. While I was at breakfast with my family."

The despair on his face makes me want to hold him all night until he forgets all about her. "Oh, come here," I say softly, pulling him into a hug.

He leans into me, his embrace tentative, as if he's not used to being comforted. We stay like that for several minutes until he pulls away.

"She got a job three hours away," he explains. "I told her I'd go with her, but she said she didn't want me to."

"Liam..."

"She's gone," he whispers, as if he's not yet come to terms with the fact. He shakes his head. "I don't want her back or anything. It's just... it's still all very new."

"I get it," I reassure him.

The oven timer goes off, bringing an end to our conversation as Liam hops up to grab the pizza.

While he cuts the pizza into slices, I find myself wondering about this ex of his. He must've been head over heels for her, but she clearly didn't feel the same way.

"It smells delicious," I tell him as he brings our dinner to the table.

"Wait until you taste it."

I pick up a slice and take a tentative bite as Liam watches me expectantly. I can barely contain my moan. "Oh my God, this is *so* good."

He picks up his own slice and takes a bite. "I've perfected the recipe over the years."

"It is perfection. You could be a chef."

"Nah, I like what I do."

"What exactly *do* you do?"

We talk about our jobs in detail over dinner, the conversation flowing freely. I want to know everything about him, but it's evident that opening up doesn't come naturally to him. Still, after only two days of getting to know one another, we've shared a fair amount of deep stuff.

I'll just have to be patient.

We finish dinner, and he loads the dishes into the dishwasher. The kitchen is warm with leftover smells of garlic. I lean against the counter beside him, completely comfortable, until he reaches into the cabinet and pulls out a bottle of whiskey.

My heart skips a beat, and the air changes. My body goes still as memories of my childhood flood my mind. Shouted curses, slammed doors.

"Did you want a glass?" he asks casually. "My dad and I always drink whiskey after dinner. It's like a tradition."

He grabs a glass, and I stare at the bottle on the counter like it's going to kill me. I want to say something to stop him, but I don't know what to say or how to explain.

He looks up and finally notes the panic on my face.

"Hey," he says gently, setting the glass down mid-motion. "Are you okay?"

I shake my head and swallow hard, my throat suddenly dry. "I'm... I can't..." My voice comes out thin.

"What's wrong?" His brow furrows with concern.

"I... get scared when men... drink whiskey," I confess, my voice barely above a whisper. "I know it's stupid. But I just don't know you that well yet," I rush out. "And we're out here alone."

He doesn't ask questions, just puts the glass back into the cabinet, a silent reassurance that he respects my boundaries. He picks up the bottle and returns it to the shelf, his movements quiet and intentional.

I take a deep breath. "It's just... when I was growing up,

my dad and uncles would drink whiskey. I remember they got really mean—"

"You don't have to explain," he says, turning to me with soft eyes. "I didn't realize."

Relief floods through me, the tension in my shoulders loosening. He grabs two beers from the fridge instead, holding one out to me. "Is this okay?

"Yeah," I answer with a smile.

"Come on," he says, nodding his head toward the back porch. "Let's get some fresh air."

I follow him, beer in hand, feeling strangely safe.

Liam and I sit on the back porch swing, rocking back and forth as the sun sets. The sounds of nature lull him to sleep, and he dozes off. His chest rises and falls steadily, and the warmth of his body next to mine comforts me.

I lift my head from his shoulder to watch him sleep peacefully. His smooth skin makes him appear young, but his full, thick beard gives him a mature look.

Twilight surrounds us, the swing rocking back and forth as the sun sets, and a couple of lightning bugs flit around the backyard, their tiny lights twinkling playfully. We're in the middle of nowhere, and I love it.

I can finally breathe, and the fresh air is invigorating. I could stay here forever, but reality tugs at the back of my mind, reminding me that I'll have to go home eventually.

Despite only knowing Liam for two days, I already feel at ease with him. He's a tough nut to crack, but I'm up to the challenge. His quiet strength and moments of gentleness draw me in, making me want to know everything about him. It's going to take some time, but after tonight, I've decided I'm in it for the long haul.

A cool breeze stirs him awake, and he looks down at me with sleepy eyes. "I guess I should take you home now."

"Are you sure you're awake enough to drive? I live kinda far."

Liam nods, but his eyes are bloodshot.

I laugh softly. "It's okay if you're too tired. I don't mind staying here tonight and heading back tomorrow, if that's okay." I suddenly panic that I'm coming on too strong, pressuring him into something he's not ready for.

"As long as you're comfortable staying, then I'd rather not drive all the way back just now. But only if you're sure you're happy staying the night. You can have my room, and I'll sleep in my parents' room."

"Yeah, that works."

Standing from the porch swing, we amble back inside, and Liam locks up and turns out the lights as I head upstairs. I'm still dressed in his old clothes, so I have to pull the pajama pants up to avoid tripping up the steps.

Once we're upstairs, he gives me a subtle once-over, but his face remains stoic as he opens his bedroom door.

I stand in the doorway and face him. "Goodnight."

"Goodnight," he says softly. He leans in and cups my jaw, kissing me on the cheek before turning and walking away.

The simple gesture sends my heart soaring, and I'm floating on air as I make my way over to the bed. A mere kiss on the cheek has my stomach doing flips, and I can't keep the grin off my face. He's the first guy in a long time to make me feel giddy.

Snuggling into the dark blue covers, I imagine Liam lying next to me. He'd wrap his arms around me, and I'd nuzzle into his neck, breathing in his masculine scent of pine and sandalwood. I wonder if Liam is picturing me right now, lying in his boyhood room, wearing his clothes. In my half-asleep state, I imagine Liam coming in here and removing them, taking charge and kissing me passionately.

I know he's nowhere near ready for that, and usually, I wouldn't be either, but I just can't help wondering how long it will be before he'll be ready to move things along with me. Figures. The one guy I'm *considering* breaking my rule for won't even kiss me.

I wake a few hours later to the sound of a distant lawnmower, and I lie there listening for a while, wondering who could possibly be mowing at this time. Peeking out the window, I realize it's Liam. He must've gotten up around five this morning to get so much of the mowing done already.

Most of the guys I know will only get up early to hit the gym. Yet Liam's already started on household chores, and it's not even six a.m. I smile to myself, admiring how hardworking he is. Now that's a *real* man.

Throwing the blanket off, I head over to the hall bathroom, only to discover that my clothes from yesterday are still damp. Looks like I'm wearing Liam's clothes home. I shimmy my shoulders excitedly at the thought of keeping something of his—a small memento of our day together.

Downstairs, I start a pot of coffee, and Liam comes in a few minutes later, grabbing an insulated cup and filling it.

"Thanks for the coffee. Ready to go?"

"Yeah," I answer sadly, heading out to the back porch for my hiking boots.

"What's wrong?" Liam asks.

"I like it here. I don't want to leave."

He smiles softly, and the sight has butterflies taking off in my chest. God his smiles are everything.

"I like it here, too. But I have to get home to my dog."

"You have a dog? I want to meet them!" I squeal, bouncing on my heels, before reality throws cold water on my face. "But I have to be at work by two."

"My house is on the way. We can stop by."

"Yay!" I practically run out the door to his truck, eager to extend our time together just a little bit longer.

Chapter 14
Liam

After locking up the house, I hop into the driver's seat of my truck. Instead of sitting in the passenger seat, Sienna slides over to the middle and buckles her seatbelt.

Her closeness gives me pause, but I don't react as I put my arm around her and back out of the driveway.

Her eyes stay on me the entire time. Apparently, the action is captivating. Not that I'm much better. It's hard to stay focused on the road when she's sitting next to me. She looks fucking incredible in my truck, even though she's wearing my shapeless clothes. The sunlight lights up her face, and her hazel eyes sparkle with excitement. I want to tell her how good she looks wearing my clothes, but I hold back. Instead, I savor the way her presence fills the cab of the truck.

Once we're on the main road, she turns to me.

"I have a confession."

"What's that?"

"I watched YouTube tutorials to learn how to bait a hook. I'd never been fishing before."

"You don't say," I drawl, more amused than anything. "Why did you say you had?"

She turns away shyly. "I wanted to be your type."

She's so fucking sweet, the corners of my lips turn up against my will. The fact that she went to such lengths to impress me has that primal feeling stirring in my chest again. *Cocky bastard.*

"But I liked fishing with you," she adds, as though feeling the need to reassure me.

"I liked it too."

We ride in comfortable silence, and I notice her staring at my forearms as I drive. I flex subtly, and her eyes travel up to my biceps. She's practically eye-fucking me, and I have a sudden fantasy of her in my bed, moaning my name as she comes.

I shake my head, trying to dispel the thought. I don't know what just came over me or how Sienna has this effect on me. I was never that way with Anna. Granted, I spent our entire relationship suppressing those urges, but still.

I clear my throat. "Do you want to listen to something else?" I ask, only now realizing what's playing through the speakers.

"Please," she laughs. "This music is depressing as hell."

"I made this playlist after Anna left me."

"Well, let's get you a new playlist."

I hand her my phone, and she opens up my music app, scrolling through some of my playlists before landing on an alternative rock one I made years ago.

"I'm surprised you like this."

"What? I can rock."

"Mm-hm. Just like you can fish?"

She laughs at my teasing. "No, I actually *do* listen to this kind of music."

I've never known someone so easy-going. I wonder whether she's always been like that or if something happened to make her that way. Part of me wants to push, to know everything about her. But I'm afraid I'll scare her off if I come on too strong, and I'm enjoying her company far too much to risk it.

We continue the drive to my house, discussing our music tastes and listening to different playlists I made. For the most part, we have similar tastes, but there are a few songs she doesn't like, and she isn't shy about telling me.

All too soon, we pull into my subdivision and I park the truck in my driveway. As we hop out and head inside, I mentally run through what I might have left out that could embarrass me. I'm pretty sure I'm in the clear, but she heads inside before I have time to hide anything.

I give her a tour of the house, which doesn't take long. It's an open-concept one-story house.

"I haven't given it much of a personal touch," I explain. "I won't be here for much longer."

She wanders into the hallway and spots an empty room with an air mattress. "A luxury guest room," she teases.

"I used to sleep in there whenever Anna stayed over."

"Wait, your ex-girlfriend, Anna?"

I nod.

She looks at me, confused. "Okay, am I missing something? Why would you stay in the guest room?"

I take a deep breath, feeling a little awkward. "She's very religious. Traditional, I guess. She wanted to wait until we were married."

"Oh," she says, surprised. "I can respect that."

Her answer surprises me, but I try not to show it. Sienna seems so vivacious, I assumed she would have more liberal opinions about sex.

We return to the kitchen, and she hops up onto the counter,

dangling her feet like she doesn't have a care in the world. I pull out a bag of mini glazed donuts from the pantry, and she lights up at the sight, sticking her hand out. I hand her the bag, and we enjoy the breakfast of champions.

"So, you two never...?"

"Never."

"Like, nothing?"

"Just kissed."

She simply nods, a hint of a smile on her face. She's looking at me like I hung the moon, but all I'm feeling is distinctly uncomfortable talking about my sex life—or lack thereof.

A scratch against the glass provides a welcome distraction, and Sienna gasps and jumps off the counter, hurrying to the back door.

"That's Zoe. She's an outside—"

Sienna slides the back door open.

"— dog."

"Aren't you just precious!" she squeals, kneeling down to pet my border collie. "Such a pretty girl."

Zoe licks her face, but Sienna doesn't seem to mind.

"How long have you had her?"

"A few months," I tell her, walking over to take Zoe onto the back porch.

I'd always planned to wait to get a dog until I moved to the farmhouse. Dogs need lots of space, and my backyard isn't quite big enough. But then Mom had started volunteering at a local animal shelter, and she'd met Zoe—a border collie puppy from a litter of rescued farm dogs. She'd decided that the little bundle of energy would be the perfect companion for me.

Sienna follows and sits on one of the chairs. I sit in the chair next to hers, and Zoe places her two front paws on me, her way of asking for pets.

As I look up from giving Zoe her requested head rubs, I find Sienna smiling softly at the two of us.

"She loves you," Sienna says. "You must be a good owner."

I shrug. "I guess." Zoe runs down the steps and into the fenced backyard. "I wish I could give her more space. Subdivision life, a tiny backyard, that's no life for a dog."

A grin brightens Sienna's face, showing off perfect straight teeth as she rests her hand on my leg, giving it a squeeze. "You've given her a home. An owner who loves her. That's a thousand times better than being stuck in a shelter."

She doesn't move her hand, but her gaze travels to the yard, where my tornado of a dog runs back and forth. I'm hyperaware of her touch, the warmth of her palm seeping through the fabric of my jeans.

"She's gonna love living at the farm," Sienna says. "You're taking her, right?"

"Of course."

We watch Zoe race around, Sienna's palm never leaving my thigh. The intimate moment lifts some of the sadness that's been weighing on my heart. Sienna's presence has been a comfort over the past three days, and for the first time in a long time, I feel a flicker of hope for the future. The farm, this new chapter of my life... with Sienna by my side, it all looks brighter.

I try to push down those feelings as soon as they surface. Hell, I've barely recovered from losing Anna; I'm not even looking for a girlfriend right now. I can't afford to get attached, especially since Sienna probably won't even stick around. She's far too bubbly and fun-loving for someone like me. She's a fun distraction, sure. But that's all she'll ever be.

Yet, as I sit here with her, I can't help but wonder if, maybe, she could be more.

Chapter 15
Liam

Back in my office on Tuesday, I find my thoughts drifting to Sienna. We shared a brief text conversation this morning, just casual small talk, but she's teaching Pilates for the next few hours, so she won't be able to reply. Even so, I find my fingers itching to pick up the phone and text her again.

I wonder what she's like as a teacher. Probably as bubbly as she is day-to-day, providing nothing but positive feedback. She invited me to come along to one of her evening classes, but only if I participate, and no matter how curious I am about her job, there's no way in hell I'm doing that.

The mental image of her in tight leggings and a sports bra, glossy hair pulled back in a ponytail, is almost too much to bear, and I have to subtly adjust my pants. I doubt I could get through watching her teach a class without getting a hard-on.

How have I only known this woman for three days? The events of the weekend make it feel like she's been in my life so much longer. I've gone from being hopelessly depressed about Anna to getting excited about a new girl. In just three days, she's had me taking her to my family farm, opening up about my break-up with Anna, lending her my clothes, introducing her to Zoe, and fantasizing about her at night. She's confident and fun and has this light, carefree way about her that makes me forget my worries, even if just for a moment.

A woman that beautiful in my childhood bed, wearing my clothes and smelling like my body wash—she would've been my teenage self's wet dream. Hell, she's my adult self's wet dream. I went to bed with a hard-on that night. But I couldn't jerk off to thoughts of her. Not when she isn't my girlfriend.

Girlfriend. I've realized over the past few days that I like the idea of her being mine, perhaps more than I should, but I know it's way too soon for that. I can't jump into a new relationship, not when my heart is still raw.

Then again, as Nathan would almost certainly say, I can't drag my feet. A girl like that won't stay single for long.

I asked her to be patient with me, and she seemed okay with taking things slow. I sigh, running my hand across my stubble. I've always rushed into relationships in the past, thinking every girl was 'the one.' But I don't want to do that this time. I need to learn from my mistakes, no matter how strong the pull is towards her.

A knock on my door jolts me out of my thoughts, and Lainey walks into my office. She always has a huge grin on her face, but I'm sure it's not real. No one can be that happy all the time.

"I have a question about the new coding program," she says, sauntering over to my desk.

She bends over next to me, but I keep my eyes on my computer screen. Her brown hair falls in my peripheral as she asks her question, and I answer it without even giving her a passing glance.

"Oh, I see. Thanks, Liam."

She sashays out of the room, and I roll my eyes. She probably already knew the answer.

I lean back in my chair and cross my arms. I find her constant attempts to get my attention irritating.

My phone vibrates on the desk, and I grab it quickly, a thrill going through me at Sienna's name on the screen.

SIENNA

My abs are on fire! The expert class kicks my butt every time.

ME

I thought you were the expert?

SIENNA

You know it! You should take the beginner's class. See me in action.

ME

While I'd love to see you in action, I'm not going to embarrass myself in front of twenty women.

SIENNA

Okay, how about just me? I could show you some moves at my apartment...

ME

I'm sure you know a lot of moves, but my body doesn't move that way.

SIENNA

At least you admit it.

ME

When can I see you again?

SIENNA

How about tonight? Come over after work.

ME

I'll be there.

A smile tugs at my lips. I'm sure I look like an idiot grinning down at my phone, but I'm alone, so I don't fight it.

The thought of spending the evening with Sienna lifts my spirits and I glance at the clock, deciding I've put in enough hours to leave early.

I can't risk Sienna changing out of her workout clothes before I get a chance to see her in them.

Chapter 16
Sienna

I'm smiling like an idiot as I message Liam, but I don't care.

I like him. A lot.

Half an hour later, Liam strides through the gym doors downstairs. The girls at the front desk point him toward the stairs, exchanging raised eyebrows and coy smiles after he walks away. I can't blame them for ogling him. He's attractive in that rugged, gruff kind of way, not like the gym bros they're used to.

He spots me on the track and falls into step next to me.

"Hi."

"Hey," he replies awkwardly, glancing around. "I've never actually been to a gym before."

I pointedly eye his biceps. "Really?"

"These muscles come from hard work. Farm life." His tone is more matter-of-fact than braggy.

I can't resist. I reach out and squeeze his bicep gently as he flexes. "Impressive." I catch a slight smile and soft pink on his cheeks before he looks away.

"How long do you usually walk for?" he asks as we amble around the track.

"Two miles, just to cool down. I'm almost done."

He nods, and I can barely hide my chuckle. It's clear he's out of his element—not just at the gym, but in the city. His jeans and cowboy boots scream that he's not from around here. I bet he doesn't even own any gym attire.

"I'm glad you're here," I add in an attempt to make him more comfortable. "You get to see 'a day in the life of Sienna'."

He keeps walking without saying a word. I guess I'm getting stoic, silent Liam today.

"After this, I usually head to the bookstore and get a coffee."

"You mean chocolate milk?" he teases.

"Yes! Mocha is the way to go."

We finish my cool down together, and I can't resist gripping his bicep again. I want to run my hands all over him.

Easy, Sienna, I tell myself. *You have to take it slow.*

As we head out of the gym, I take his arm and guide us down the street, dodging oncoming pedestrians. Liam's muscles tense under my fingers every time someone passes too close, but eventually, we arrive at the local bookstore cafe.

Entering the quiet sanctuary, I lead us to the back, where I order my usual, and Liam opts for a mocha cold brew, paying for both. My mouth falls open in shock for a second before I slam it closed, my heart warming at the fact that he took my recommendation.

"Thanks for the coffee. Again." I watch for any reaction as he takes the first sip, but as usual, he gives nothing away. "Well, what do you think?" I ask, bouncing on my heels.

"It's actually pretty good," he says, though he doesn't smile.

Grinning, I take his arm again, and we wander through the aisles with our drinks as I pick out a few books.

I love this place. The books are all pre-loved, and the whole space smells of paper and coffee. Plus, everything is a bargain, and your girl is on a budget.

We sit at a table near the window, and Liam shuffles through my stack of books, reading the titles out loud.

"*Hearts of the Open Range; Lassoed by Love; Saddle Up, Sweetheart; Whispers of the Wild West; Cowboy's Tender Touch*." He shakes his head. "You have a type."

He picks one at random and skims a page. His eyes go wide as he reads a passage to himself. "*This* is what you read?"

"Uh-huh," I say, sipping my drink.

"It's basically porn," he whispers, leaning forward as though he's afraid of someone overhearing us.

I roll my eyes. "They're romance novels. I read them for the plot."

"The plot?" He flips the book over and reads the synopsis. "*City girl Emma Dawson inherits a Montana ranch and finds herself in over her head, until rugged cowboy Jake Carson steps in. As they work side by side, the chemistry between them ignites into a blazing passion.*"

"You can borrow it when I'm done," I tease.

He shakes his head. "I can't believe I'm about to spend money on this."

My brows knit in confusion.

"You didn't think I'd let you pay for your books, did you?"

I brace myself for Liam's reaction as I unlock my apartment door. We step inside, and he looks around before taking his boots off.

"It's not much," I warn him, feeling a bit embarrassed.

"It's nice," he replies, probably just to be polite.

Ever since I got back from the farm, my studio apartment

has felt suffocatingly tiny. I keep it minimalist to avoid clutter, so the counters are practically bare. I decorated the apartment in creams and whites with gold accents, and I light candles often, so the entire apartment smells like a bakery.

Liam follows me to my room, where I place my books on the small white bookshelf. A queen-sized bed under the only window dominates the space. A large mirror on the opposite wall reflects the window's light, creating the illusion of more room and making the space feel a little bigger and brighter. Sheer white curtains add to the airy feel.

"Ta-da," I say, spreading my arms.

He nods and looks around. "I like what you've done to the place."

I sigh as I sit on the bed. "It feels like a coffin compared to your farm."

"It certainly smells better than my farm," he jokes.

I expect him to sit next to me on the bed, but instead, he remains standing, legs spread out and thumbs in his belt loops. I slowly drag my gaze up and down his tall, lean body. He exudes a seductive, confident presence that makes my exes look like boys compared to him.

Not that there have been many. I've only had one man in this room, and I've regretted it for years.

Liam's deep voice shakes me out of my thoughts.

"I thought I'd take you out to dinner tonight."

"That sounds nice." I look in the mirror at my matching sports bra and leggings. "I guess I should change first."

He steps out to give me privacy, closing the door behind him.

Gentlemanly *and* rugged. It's a heady combination.

Ten minutes later, I emerge in a bright white sundress and platform sandals, my hair falling in waves down my back.

"You look nice," Liam says, walking towards me.

Without thinking, I wrap my arms around him, and he only hesitates for a few seconds before hugging me back. With my heels, I come up to his chin, allowing me to rest my cheek against his chest.

Though I can't tell for sure, I sense his lips brushing softly against my hair, and I feel his chest rise as he takes a deep inhale.

"Are you... smelling me?" I ask, lifting my head to meet his eyes.

"No," he says awkwardly. "Not on purpose." I burst out laughing.

"You do smell really good, though."

I laugh even harder. "So do you. In a manly way." I blush. "That sounded bad." I let go and step back. "Ready to go?"

"Lead the way."

Chapter 17
Sienna

"I'm seriously impressed," Liam says as we walk through the door of my apartment two hours later.

"I told you the food there is amazing."

"I meant with you." He sits in a chair to take off his boots. "How does a woman your size put away that much food?"

I shrug and remove my sandals. "A girl's gotta eat."

"A half-pound burger, fries, and ten hot wings?"

"With room for dessert," I tease. "With how much I exercise, I can eat whatever I want."

"I figured. Still, it's impressive."

I wrap my arms around his neck and hug him. "Thanks for dinner," I say softly. "Do you want to stay?"

The sudden tension in his body gives away his nerves, but he responds with a casual, "Sure."

I don't want to push, but I don't want him to leave either, so I suggest a movie and drinks.

"I'd like that," he says, moving to the couch.

"Pick whatever you want," I tell him from the kitchen.

I take out two martini glasses and drizzle rich chocolate fudge sauce inside. Then I pour vodka and chocolate liqueur into a cocktail shaker and give it a good shake over my shoulder, pouring the mixture into the glasses. Finally, I top the drinks with marshmallow creme and crushed graham crackers.

Carrying them to the living room, I sit down carefully, handing one to Liam. "I call it a S'more-tini. I should warn you, they're pretty strong."

"I can handle myself," he assures me. He takes a sip, licking his lips—his soft, perfectly sculpted lips. "That's really good. I'm impressed again."

I sip my own drink, looking at him over the rim of my glass. "I'm somewhat of a novice bartender."

"Wow. You can't even taste the alcohol," Liam says, already halfway through his drink.

"I'll take that as a compliment."

The movie starts, and I shuffle closer to him on the couch, relaxing after a long day. Around halfway through, I head back to the kitchen to make us two more. I sit back down and savor my drink a little more this time, carefully sipping the rich flavors, but Liam practically gulps his down.

His eyes become slightly glossed over from the alcohol. Smiles and laughs that don't usually come easily to him bubble out of him as the movie continues. The thought of Liam feeling comfortable enough to let go of some of that stoic demeanor makes me want to kick my feet, but I restrain myself.

As the credits roll, we set our empty glasses on the coffee table, and Liam leans back against the couch, closing his eyes. I scoot closer to him, and he slowly opens his eyes and turns his head until our noses almost touch.

"Are you an angel?" he asks as he gazes into my eyes.

I giggle, and he cups my cheek, his breath sweet against my lips.

"I'm serious. You're perfect. I think you're an angel." His eyes dart over my face. "You are so beautiful. And you smell like a vanilla cupcake. You smell fuc—really delectable."

Mirroring his smile, I whisper, "Maybe I *am* an angel."

"That's the only exclamation," he slurs.

"Exclamation?" I chuckle.

"You're fuc—really gorgeous."

His brown eyes roam over my white dress down to my tan legs, then to my bare feet. His eyes linger on my cleavage on the way back up to my eyes.

"You're so pure," he whispers.

I can't help but laugh. "I'm not pure. Trust me."

"Shh," he says, placing a finger against my lips. "You are to me."

I feel my eyes start to water, my throat suddenly painful. "I'm not like your ex."

"I don't want you to be," he says, suddenly serious. "I like you how you are."

"I like you too," I whisper, our lips drawing closer.

For a moment, I think he might close the distance between our lips, but he simply continues to stare into my eyes.

"When I'm with you, I forget about all the other sh—stuff."

I let out a giggle. "Why don't you cuss around me?"

"My dad taught me that a gentleman never curses at a lady."

I shift my body closer, pressing my hand to his upper thigh, my heart thumping in my chest. "Maybe I like your dirty mouth."

He closes the distance, enveloping me with his body, his soft lips finally meeting my own. The velvet of his mouth contrasts with the scratch of his scruff against my cheeks, and I smile through the kiss.

He nudges my body backward gently, laying me down until he's on top of me, his lips never leaving mine. He tastes like s'mores and vodka, and I fucking love it. I spread my legs, and he rests his weight on top of me, the hardness of his cock pressing against my core through our clothes.

His lips move to my neck, softly caressing the skin with each kiss, and I can't hold back my moan. I'm practically quivering with anticipation, my lips curving in a mischievous smile. He lifts his head to look into my eyes, his own eyes reflecting unspoken desire. He closes them again, pressing a gentle, reassuring kiss to my lips before blinking slowly, like he's waking up from a dream.

He jumps off the couch.

"I... Shi— sorry, I shouldn't have... The alcohol..." He shakes his head. "I should go," he says, sounding disappointed.

"You don't have to apologize. I enjoyed it. Besides, you shouldn't drive," I pause, reaching out for his hand and giving him a reassuring squeeze. "Why don't you stay here tonight?"

He nods, running his other hand through his hair. "You're right. Is that alright? I can take the couch—"

"No, it's okay." I stand, reaching for his other hand so I can pull him closer. "My bed is big enough for both of us. You can stay with me."

Chapter 18
Liam

My head swims as I close the bedroom door behind me, trying to get my bearings as I stare at Sienna standing in the center of the room. I should have heeded her warning when she said that the drink was strong. Four shots of vodka in quick succession, and I'm no longer acting like myself.

Sienna brushes her hair to one side and glances over her shoulder at me. Stepping closer, I tentatively grasp the zipper of her dress, pausing as I reevaluate whether this is actually what she wants or just what I'm projecting onto the situation. She gives me a nod of reassurance, encouraging me to slowly pull it down, exposing the bare expanse of her back. I'm careful not to touch her, not even a brush of my fingertips.

We linger like that, my eyes catching our reflections in the mirror on the wall. Desire stirs within me. I want to go further with her, and it's not just because of the alcohol in my system. But I'm not ready to jump into another relationship, and I don't want to give Sienna the wrong idea.

Sienna slowly reaches up, lowering the straps of her dress down her shoulders. I'm so close I can see a light dusting of freckles, and I want to kiss each one. Just as she's about to let the dress fall, I turn and head into the bathroom.

Leaning against the door, I take deep breaths and try to sober up. I fill a cup with water from the sink and gulp it down, taking a minute to look around. It's a typical woman's bathroom. Lotions and skincare in a basket on the back of the toilet. Makeup placed neatly in an organizer on the small counter.

Feeling slightly more grounded, I open the door. Sienna's already in bed, wearing comfy sweats and a cropped tank top that shows off a little cleavage and an inch of her belly. She's so fucking adorable I want to wrap my arms around her and never let go.

The overhead light is off now, replaced by the soft glow of a lamp, creating an intimate ambiance. I regret those two mixed drinks right about now. Don't get me wrong, I want to sleep next to her, but there's an implication there that I'm not ready for.

She snuggles under the thick comforter, pulling it down on the other side, inviting me in. It's an innocent move, but sleeping next to someone holds its own intimacy.

I approach with a slight hesitancy, and she props herself up on her elbows.

"You can take your jeans off," she says quietly.

I stop in my tracks. They are pretty tight, and I'd sleep better in my underwear.

"Are you sure?"

She smiles and nods, so I unbutton them and slide the zipper down, feeling her gaze on me. She watches while I slowly step out of my jeans, her appreciative gaze giving me the courage to grab the back of my shirt and pull it over my head.

I climb in next to her and pull the blanket up. The queen-sized bed offers plenty of space for both of us to sleep comfortably, yet my body goes stiff as she turns on her side to face me.

"Good night," she whispers.

"Good night." I reach for the lamp, but she stops me, guiding my hand to her waist, my pinkie grazing her bare skin.

Laying like this gives her an exaggerated hourglass figure. She's the epitome of sexiness, and my body responds. I'm growing harder by the second from the barest of touches.

"Sienna," I whisper.

She shakes her head, cupping my jaw. Her warm, petal-soft lips meet mine for just a second, making my cock harden all the way.

Her closeness has caused something in me to awaken, and my arousal is undeniable. Four days with this woman, and already my need for her is painfully evident. It's not just her body; it's everything about her. I've never felt such passion, such desire for a person, and it scares me.

Sienna kisses me again, moving closer. As much as I want her body pressed against mine, I don't want her to feel my erection. I pull away from the kiss and turn away.

If she's disappointed, she doesn't show it.

We lie there, both of us breathing a little heavier than normal. The space between us does nothing to soften the hardness between my legs. I struggle to steady my racing heart, but her presence is too much.

Eventually, she falls asleep, her soft breathing the only sound in the room. The light from the lamp casts a gentle glow over her, and I take in her features. Her long eyelashes rest against her cheeks, and her smooth skin gives her a youthful glow.

I watch her sleep like a fucking weirdo, but I can't help it. I don't want to look away. She could have any guy she wants, yet she chose me to share her bed. I wonder what she wanted those kisses to lead to, how far she wanted to go with me.

It doesn't matter. We've both been drinking, and I'm not ready to be her boyfriend, not yet. Besides, she deserves better than a drunken tumble in the sheets.

Sienna's breathing becomes heavier, slowing as she falls into a deep sleep, and I take the opportunity to get some space from her. I slowly slip out of bed and head back into the bathroom. Keeping the light off so as not to wake her, I glance at myself in the mirror in the dim light coming through the window.

The effects of the alcohol are wearing off, but the effects of Sienna run rampant. I stand there, cock fully erect and straining against my underwear. I grip the countertop and take deep breaths, willing this erection to go away. My need for release doesn't let up, and I resign myself to the fact that I will have to take care of it.

I don't want to, but my cock is insistent. I turn away from the mirror and pull my dick out. Closing my eyes, I grip it firmly and begin to stroke, remembering how good it felt to kiss Sienna and lay her down on the couch. How I lowered my body onto hers and positioned myself between her legs. She'd spread her legs for me, giving me access to her panties—if she was wearing any under that white dress.

I'm lost in the fantasy as I continue to fuck my own hand, moving my palm up and down my shaft as quietly as I can.

Avoiding my reflection, I face the shower. The shower. Where Sienna stands every day, naked under hot water, rubbing herself with soap and running her hands over her body.

Without thinking, I step into the shower, stroking my cock

all the while.

I spot her body wash, and I can't help myself. I open the lid and hold it under my nose, the coconut scent almost hurtling me over the edge. She's not even here with me, and I'm still undone by her scent; that's how intoxicating she is. I'm feeling reckless and electrified, and I turn the bottle over and squeeze it over my rock-hard length, stroking with increasing urgency, spreading the body wash over my cock. Finally, I come, sending hot spurts down the shower drain.

My breath comes in ragged gasps, and I pray to God I didn't wake Sienna. Once my breathing calms down, I step out of the shower. Staring at myself in the mirror, I'm disgusted. Ashamed.

I feel like a fucking creep masturbating to the thought of Sienna. She trusts me. We're getting to know each other as friends.

I shake my head, shoving my soft dick back inside my underwear before sneaking out of the bathroom silently.

I breathe a sigh of relief that Sienna is down for the count. Gathering my clothes, I take one last look at her before I turn off the lamp. I regret that I won't get to see her lit up by the early morning light. I bet she's even more beautiful with the soft rays of dawn streaming in through the window.

Shame takes over, and I turn away from her sleeping form.

I don't deserve to see it.

How would Sienna react if she knew what I had just done in her shower? Would she be revolted? Angry?

I quickly dress myself in the living room before heading out, feeling sick over what I just did. I drive home in silence, berating myself the entire way.

Chapter 19
Sienna

It's been three days since Liam stayed the night at my apartment. Since then, I've gotten nothing from him other than short texts. They're not cold, just polite. The worst part is, we have no plans to see each other again.

He's all I can think about as Veronica and I wander through a resale clothing store, sifting through racks of clothes. She holds up a blue and yellow flower-patterned tank top, but all I can bring myself to do is nod and smile.

My thoughts drift back to Liam. I'd thought everything was great, that we were making progress with whatever this is between us. We'd flirted, kissed, cuddled... he'd even said he wanted to explore this.

Had I read things wrong? Having him sleep over must have been too much too soon.

As I browse a rack of dresses, I try to see things from his perspective. His ex-girlfriend didn't want to share a bed with him. All they'd ever done was kiss. Four days with me, and we'd already almost gone further. He's probably overwhelmed.

V holds out an olive-green bikini. "It's so cute, but it's too big for me. You should try it on, Sienna."

I take it from her and add it to my pile.

I'm disappointed that Liam hasn't asked to see me again, but I understand his need for space. Things are moving pretty fast between us. It'd be smart to keep our distance. It still stings, though.

V puts on a light-pink ball cap and holds a pair of cotton shorts against her hips, the color matching perfectly.

"How do you do that?"

"It's a gift!"

I shake my head and continue browsing, drawn to a rack of white tops, my signature color.

"You look so good in white," V sighs. "I'm so jealous of your tan." She holds up a white tank top against me. "I just burn and peel." She adds it to her own pile.

"You're jealous of *me*? You can wear *anything* and make it look adorable as hell. You're like a fairy."

She rolls her eyes good-naturedly and moves to a different rack, showing me a tiny yellow romper.

"I hope you picked that for yourself—that thing would give me a wedgie up to my cervix."

We both laugh, and she adds it to her try-on pile.

A little while later, we take our finds into the dressing rooms. V talks in the stall next to mine about what fits and what doesn't. If something is too big for her, she tosses it over the wall to me, and vice versa.

"I like this white top, but you can totally see my nipples. Can I borrow your white bra?" she asks.

"Sorry, I left it at—" I stop myself.

"Left it where?"

I remain silent, hoping she forgets what I said.

"Left it *where*?" she repeats.

Before I can respond, V is crawling under the gap between our stalls, standing to her full height, a head shorter than me.

"Sienna Elizabeth Machlan, you tell me right now where you left that bra," she demands sternly.

I giggle at such might coming from such a small person. I shrug casually. "I met someone."

"You *met* someone?!" she whisper-screams. "Like, a guy?"

"Oh, he's a *man*."

She bounces on her heels. "Tell me everything!"

"Do we have to do this here? You're at eye level with my tits right now."

"Fine." She sighs. "But I want to know every detail!"

Veronica and I settle onto the couch in my apartment, wrapped in cozy sweatshirts and shorts, blankets draped over our legs to ward off the chill of the apartment.

We face each other on the couch, cocktails in hand, made by yours truly: strawberry soda, Malibu rum, and cut-up strawberries because I'm extra. A concoction as vibrant and sweet as the girl sitting across from me.

"Okay, okay, okay," V says, eyes wide with excitement. "You've edged me long enough. What's his name?"

"Liam," I reply, not bothering to hide my smile. "He's so..." I shake my head, searching for the right word. "I don't even know."

She squeals and kicks her feet. "I'm so happy for you! Should we invite Chloe and Amber over?"

I shake my head. "Let's just keep this between us for now."

"Why?"

"I don't know. I just... I've only known him a week, and

he's the first guy I've liked in a long time. I don't want them to hound me about it."

"Okay, fine. My lips are sealed. So tell me about him!"

"Well... he's a country boy. He's going to inherit a farm when he turns twenty-five, and he's not very comfortable in the city."

"I gave a country boy a chance once. His hands were always so dirty." V grimaces. "Like, permanently dirty."

"Well, my man's not like the boys you're used to. He's distinguished. Mature."

"I like what I'm hearing."

I chuckle and pull up his Instagram.

"And I like what I'm seeing!"

"He took me to his farm, and we spent the whole day together." I smile wistfully. "We fell into the pond, so we had to shower—"

She raises her eyebrows.

"Separately!" I clarify, a blush spreading on my cheeks. "Nothing sexual happened. Unless you count cooking me dinner as foreplay."

"Aww, he cooked you dinner?" she says, placing a hand over her heart.

"Homemade pizza. From *scratch*. From scratch, V!"

"Ugh. Why can't I find a guy like that?"

"Oh, it gets better. He has the most adorable dog in the world—Zoe. And when he took me to the bookstore..."

Her eyes go wide.

"... he bought my books for me!"

She throws herself down on the couch dramatically. "I would die."

We giggle like schoolgirls gushing over a boy, the effects of our drinks taking hold.

"I just like him so much! I could talk about him all day."

"I love that for you. You deserve someone like him." She sips her drink with a dreamy look in her eye. "When are you gonna see him again?"

"I don't know," I say, disappointment creeping into my voice. "We went to dinner after our bookstore date, then we kissed on the couch—things got pretty steamy. He even slept in my bed that night, but he left before I woke up. I haven't seen him in person in three days."

We finish our cocktails and set the empty glasses on the table.

"Maybe it's moving too fast for him. I think staying the night was too much."

"I've never heard of a guy thinking sexual things are moving too fast."

I shake my head. "He's not like that. His ex-girlfriend wanted to wait until marriage. He dated her for months, and they never had sex."

She drapes her legs over my lap and lies down. "Hold on to him, Sienna. He sounds like one of the good ones."

"Shit, I'm sorry, V. Thinking about Marcus?"

"No, fuck him. I'm over it. You don't need to worry about me."

"Good."

I rest my head back on the couch, feeling flushed from the alcohol. Or maybe it's because I'm talking about Liam.

I don't want to push him; I'm trying to give him space. But I can't help wanting to see him.

"Why don't you invite Liam out to the bar with us tomorrow night?" V suggests. "It's a group setting, so it's more casual than a date."

I consider her idea for a moment. "Well, I would like to see if he gets along with you all... Okay, I'll ask him."

Chapter 20
Sienna

The dimly lit bar pulses with energy as the thumping bass reverberates through the air. I nurse my rum punch, the tropical sweetness marred by the bartender's heavy pour. The smoky atmosphere and loud music envelop me as I watch the door. Liam said he'd be here, but he didn't say when.

Perched on a high-top chair, I let my feet dangle as I wait for him to arrive. I can't believe how much I've missed him. I have to play it cool, though, especially in front of my friends. I'd never hear the end of it.

When he finally walks through the door, I have to restrain myself from running over to hug him, opting for a wave instead. He gives me a slight nod but no smile back.

As he orders a drink at the bar, I wonder if I've done something wrong. Sure, Liam's been stoic most of the time we've spent together, but we've barely spoken for three days. I'd expected at least a hint that he's happy to see me.

He doesn't even glance my way while waiting for his drink, an impenetrable mask in place on his face by the time he heads over to our table with his beer.

I make quick introductions, but Liam stays silent, barely acknowledging my friends. I try to keep my anxiety and frustration in check. We're off to a rocky start, but there's still time to salvage the night.

"Do you want to try my drink?" I ask him, hoping the reference to our first date will at least make him smile.

He shakes his head.

"So, what do you do?" Amber asks, trying to make conversation.

"Software engineering," he mutters.

We sit through the next couple of songs, chatting amongst ourselves, but the initial awkwardness lingers. Liam looks like he'd rather be anywhere but here. Why did he come if he's just going to sit here in silence?

I try to keep the conversation going, recounting funny stories with the girls that have us all laughing—except Liam. His guarded demeanor remains in place, in stark contrast to the animated chatter around us.

I lean closer to him. "Do you want to go somewhere and talk?"

"I need another drink," he says, jumping off his seat to head back to the bar.

It stings, but I give him the benefit of the doubt.

"Is he just gonna sit there and scowl all night?" Chloe says rudely.

I reign in my anger. "He's not scowling. He's..." I trail off, realizing she's right. That's exactly what he was doing. "This just isn't his scene."

"Whatever."

I hop off my chair and head toward Liam at the bar.

"Is something wrong?" I ask.

He doesn't answer.

The frustration that's been building all night finally comes to a head. "You don't have to be rude to my friends."

He takes a deep breath and nods. "I'm sorry. I'll try to talk to them."

"Thank you."

The bartender heads our way, and I order a bay breeze, which Liam pays for. Once we have our drinks, we return to the table, and I try to steer the conversation towards something Liam can engage with.

"Amber is thinking of getting a dog for her boys. Do you think she should get a border collie, like Zoe?"

"That depends," Liam says, addressing Amber. "They're very energetic, so they need space to run, and they need to be walked often."

"So do my boys," Amber jokes.

Liam's lips tilt up a fraction, and I feel like I've won the lottery. "But they're really smart and loyal, so they'd make a great first dog."

Liam's earlier tension eases as he makes small talk with Amber. I smile to myself as I sip my bay breeze—made with orange juice instead of pineapple juice. God, can't they get anything right?

I leave Liam with my friends and head to the jukebox. Scrolling through the songs on the screen, I pick one I know will get my friends to the dance floor.

When it starts playing, my friends join me and some other girls on the dance floor in the middle of the bar. The energy flows, and we move in sync, our bodies swaying to the rhythm of the music. I'm never happier than when I'm dancing with my friends. It reminds me of our old cheerleading days.

We throw our hands in the air and sway our hips, catching the attention of a few guys. Laughter and smiles light up my friends' faces as we move to the beat. As the song ends and another plays, we stay on the dance floor, the four of us standing in a circle and swaying to the music with drinks in hand.

I glance over at Liam, now seated on a chair against the wall. I want him to come and dance with me, but I know that's not going to happen. My man prefers to be on the sidelines, and that's fine by me.

"So that's your guy, huh?" Amber asks.

"Yeah," I say dreamily. "Isn't he cute?"

"Yeah, if you're into Woody," Chloe quips.

I stop dancing. "What the fuck did you just say?"

She doesn't take me seriously. "Come on," she says with a laugh. "He's wearing fucking cowboy boots. Are you serious?"

"I happen to find them sexy," I snap. "In fact, I plan on taking them off him tonight."

I don't stick around for their reaction. I storm over to Liam—why did he have to wear a plaid shirt today?—and take his arm.

"Let's get out of here."

"Gladly," he replies.

We walk past my friends on the dance floor on our way to the exit.

"Have fun with your toy," Chloe calls after us.

I give her the finger without looking back.

I storm out of the bar and down the street, arms crossed over my chest.

Liam catches up to me in two strides of his long legs, turning me around to guide me toward his truck in the parking lot.

"What was that about? 'Have fun with your toy'?"

I shake my head. "You don't want to know." I'm still seething with anger at Chloe for making fun of my boyf— Liam. "Let's just go."

He opens the passenger side door and helps me in. Tears sting my eyes as he walks around the front and hops in.

"What's wrong?" he asks quietly.

"Fucking Chloe. She always does that. Any time someone is happy, she has to shit all over it."

"Do you want to go home?"

"Please."

I press my palms against my eyelids to stem the tears as he pulls out of the parking lot and drives toward my apartment. God, I can't wait for the day that box isn't my home anymore.

Wiping at my eyes, I watch the streetlights cast elongated shadows across Liam's profile, highlighting the furrow of his brow as he navigates the city. I decide it's as good a time as any to find out what's been bothering him.

"Why were you so grumpy tonight?" I ask, my throat tight from holding back tears.

"I don't like crowds. People."

"I should hope not. You're about to live a million miles away from civilization."

"I like it that way."

We ride in silence until he parks outside my apartment.

I turn to him, finally calm enough to voice the question I've really been wanting to ask. "Why did you come tonight? You left before I woke up the other day, and you've barely spoken to me the last three days."

He stares forward, as if asking himself the same question. "Because I can't stay away from you."

I'm speechless. Liam seems as perturbed by his statement as I am, and it takes him a moment to shift his gaze to meet mine. The intensity of his expression has my heart fluttering in my chest.

"I was trying to give you space."

"I don't want it. I want you." His voice is tinged with a note of desperation.

Hope burns through my veins, and I unbuckle my seatbelt, sliding across the leather to straddle him. "I want you too," I whisper.

He accepts my kiss, but it's not full of the same passion as our kiss the other night.

Pulling away, I wrap my arms around his neck, taking in the tortured look on his face. I press my forehead to his. "What's wrong? You can talk to me."

"I want to be with you. But I need time to figure out my feelings."

My heart sinks. "I can make you forget her," I murmur softly, cupping his face.

"This isn't about her. I'm not ready for another relationship. I can't give you what you want. What we both want. Not yet."

I can't stop the tears that fill my eyes, obscuring my vision.

"Sienna, I'm sorry. God, I wish I could just... You have to understand. My whole life, I've jumped headfirst into relationships. I fall hard and fast, and I don't want to do that with you. I don't want to rush this."

The tears fall, and I drop my hands from his face. Liam

wipes the tears away with his thumbs.

"I like you, Sienna. A lot. More than I've ever liked anyone. But I want to do this right. I want us to get to know each other first. As friends."

I glance out of his window, trying to focus on the positives. Liam might not be ready for a romantic relationship, but he showed up tonight to meet my friends despite hating crowds. He's been nothing but honest with me, even when I didn't like the truth. Most importantly, he opened up about his vulnerabilities, his worries. He's shown a level of maturity I'm not used to but one I want to cling to. No matter what our relationship looks like.

"I suppose I can do that."

Chapter 21
Liam

Soft rays of sunshine stream through white curtains, reflecting off the large gold mirror on the opposite wall. Sienna's room is tiny, but she makes creative use of the space. I can see her vision: she uses white and cream-colored blankets and rugs, gold accents, sheer curtains, and minimal clutter to give the place a light and airy feel. It's warm and inviting, despite its small size, unlike the cold emptiness of my own home.

The windowsill holds six candles, each exuding a fragrance of a different baked good or dessert. The sun's warmth has heated up the wax, releasing subtle scents that add to the cozy ambiance. However, I have to admit that the dominant scent of Cinnamon Donut is making my stomach growl.

I stare at the ceiling. Mom will be upset I'm missing church this morning, but I couldn't resist staying over when Sienna invited me to stay last night. I missed the chance to see Sienna sleeping in the morning light. I wouldn't make that mistake again. Besides, Mom would be ecstatic if she knew I was seeing someone again.

I haven't told anyone about Sienna yet. I'm not ready to share this part of my life. I just hope this thing between Sienna and me lasts long enough for me to tell my family about us.

I take a moment to admire Sienna's ethereal beauty: the radiance of her skin in the gentle glow of sunrise; the softness of her lips parted in sleep; the innocence of her face, relaxed as she dreams; the shine of her hair spread out on the pillow.

My gaze travels further down. Her matching pink pajama set shows off her toned, slender body, her hard muscles complementing her soft, feminine curves.

I brush away a strand of hair and place a gentle kiss on her forehead. As she stirs awake, I pull away, reminding myself that we've decided to take this slow and get to know each other as friends first.

"It's too early to get out of bed," she mumbles.

I smile at the sound of her voice, rough from sleep. "Your candle is making my stomach growl," I explain, moving to sit up.

She wraps her hand around mine and pulls me back down. "You're warm," she murmurs, nuzzling her face into my neck and molding her body against mine.

I freeze for a second, but I'm too weak to resist. I wrap my arms around her and try to rationalize the action, telling myself that some people cuddle their friends, but a snarky voice inside my head insists that I'm kidding myself.

I shove the voice down, relaxing into Sienna's warmth.

We lay like that until my stomach growls audibly.

"Okay," Sienna concedes, giggling. "We can get up now."

I leave the warmth of the bed and put my clothes back on, the same ones I wore yesterday, before heading into the bathroom to use some of Sienna's mouthwash.

When I join Sienna in the kitchen, she's still in that cotton tank top and short shorts, and I can't tear my eyes away from her body as she moves gracefully around the kitchen. She's effortlessly beautiful, even without makeup.

She pours a chocolate protein shake and a coffee-flavored one into a blender, adding a scoop of protein powder.

She turns to me as it blends. "Do you want one?"

"I usually get my protein from meat, but sure."

I take a seat at the small table as she pours the mixture over ice and hands it to me, watching as I take a tentative sip. The artificial chocolate and coffee flavors flow over my tongue. I have to rely on my years of mastering self-control not to grimace at the taste.

"It's not bad. Just a little gritty."

She chuckles, and the rich tone of her morning laughter makes me feel things in places I should definitely not be.

"You get used to it. I have one of these every morning."

The knowledge makes me want to show her what a decent breakfast looks like, to cook for her every morning so she never has to go to work with only gross protein coffee to sustain her. I shove that thought down.

She quickly makes another and sits down with her own cup, sipping it slowly as we enjoy the tranquility of Sunday morning. It's my favorite time of day—the quiet of sunrise. There's nothing better than enjoying the peace of morning, letting the world wait a little longer.

As the sun rises higher, brightening up the apartment, Sienna takes notice of my nearly full cup.

She gives me a look. "You don't have to drink it."

"Oh, thank God," I say, pushing it across the table to her. "I can't believe you drink that every morning."

She shrugs. "I need a lot of protein. A body like this comes with a lot of maintenance."

"I get that, but you're missing out on one of the best parts about drinking coffee in the morning."

"And what would that be?"

"The aroma of freshly brewed coffee waking you up."

"I have a candle for that," she says, jumping up and moving to a bottom cabinet in the kitchen. She digs around until she finds a large candle. Grabbing a match from the drawer, she sets the coffee bean-patterned candle on the table and lights it.

I turn the candle to read the name: *Espresso Cake Pop*.

"Not exactly what I had in mind... Just how many candles do you have?"

She grabs my hand and drags me upright, opening the cabinet doors to reveal an impressive collection of at least thirty candles.

"Wow."

"Yeah... I can't help it. I love lighting sweet-smelling candles. They're so pretty!"

She pulls out one labeled *Chocolate Chip Cookies*. Taking off the lid, she holds it under her nose and breathes in.

"And they smell so good," she says, holding the candle under my nose.

I can't help but smile at her enthusiasm for such an innocent obsession.

She has me smell a few more candles before my stomach growls again.

She laughs softly. "Let's get you some real food."

As the day wears on, Sienna and I sink into an easy comfort with each other. There's none of the usual awkwardness that comes when you first start seeing someone. Though I suppose we're not exactly 'seeing each other'.

I teach her how to cook an omelet, and she shares her book collection with me, pointing out a few favorites and recommending some I might like. We sift through old photos as she recounts stories about her friends and family, each one offering a glimpse into her life.

Morning fades into afternoon as we lay on her bed, our bodies relaxed and conversation flowing. Her hand finds mine, intertwining our fingers naturally as we talk. The outside world seems to disappear as we lose ourselves in conversation.

Sienna's genuine interest and curiosity draw me out, and I open up more than I ever have. I find myself sharing experiences I usually keep to myself. I can feel myself getting closer to her, not only physically but emotionally.

Her head rests on my chest as I talk about my high school days. I wasn't exactly popular, but I had a lot of friends. She tells me about her own high school days, and I gather she and her friends were in a popular clique. Despite our different backgrounds, we find common ground in shared experiences.

Afternoon blends into evening, and I marvel at our easy intimacy as we get to know each other. I trace lazy patterns on her shoulder as she tells me about her dreams for the future. She wants to get out of the city and live on a big piece of land. She doesn't want kids right away; instead, she wants to explore different careers. Her ambition and sense of adventure intrigue me, and I can only hope she wants me around for her future.

We order in for dinner, eating on the couch as Sienna introduces me to a new show. It's a teen drama mystery about four girls being stalked and harassed by a mysterious person.

I roll my eyes at first, but by the second episode, I'm hooked.

After spending the entire day together, I'm still not tired of her. In fact, I want to stay the night again, but I have work tomorrow. I can't call off just because I want to hang out with her. She has classes to teach anyway.

Sienna hugs me at the door, and I resist the urge to kiss her as I reluctantly head out. I'm glad we talked things out last night and agreed to take things slow. After the day we had together, it's clear we're heading towards more than friendship.

We're somewhere in between, and I like where we are.

Chapter 22
Sienna

Sitting on a bench with Amber, I bask in the summer sun. Her boys run around the playground like lunatics, playing some game where the rules change every two minutes. I tried to keep up with them, but their energy and wildness were too much to handle.

"Liam and I have seen each other every day this week," I gush to Amber. "We either hang out at my apartment or his house. Sometimes he takes me out to dinner, sometimes he cooks."

"Uh-huh," Amber murmurs, her eyes fixed on the boys.

"We text about everything, even while he's at work. Everything just feels so natural with him. We can sit in silence and simply enjoy each other's company."

"Mm-hm."

Despite my determination to stay upbeat, her terse responses are beginning to cast a shadow over my excitement, but I continue to ramble on like a love-sick schoolgirl.

"He's so hardworking and smart and mature. And he's a damn good cook, too."

Silence. Not even a nod.

"And he bought me books," I add, hoping to finally elicit a reaction.

Nothing.

"Jeez, I at least thought him buying me books would impress you, if nothing else."

She doesn't respond, and I finally start to get angry. No 'I'm happy for you'. No 'I'm glad you found someone'. Nothing. It's a stark contrast to my conversation with V last weekend.

As the conversation dwindles, an uncomfortable silence settles between us, thick with unspoken tension. Amber side-eyes me before returning her gaze to the playground with a scowl. Her crossed arms and furrowed brow speak volumes, her disapproval clear without a word spoken.

I wait for her to start talking, but she remains silent.

"Is everything okay?" I eventually ask. Normally if something is wrong, she opens up about it.

To my surprise, she just shrugs. "I guess," she says, giving a pointed glance at my form-fitting tank top.

I follow her gaze down to my outfit: the tank top is one of my favorites—a warm tan color that complements my sun-kissed skin, clinging to my frame in a way that subtly accentuates my waist and cleavage—and my cotton shorts show off the long, tan legs I've worked hard to keep in shape.

"Do you *have* to wear that?" she says, her tone edged with disapproval.

"Why shouldn't I?" I reply casually, completely unbothered by her judgment of my clothes. I wear what I want.

She rolls her eyes. "We're at a park. Who are you trying to impress?"

"No one, I just like this outfit. I take pride in the way I look."

"As opposed to me," she says bitterly.

She's wearing an oversized t-shirt, probably her boyfriend's, and worn leggings. Her hair sits on top of her head in a messy bun. Sure, her eyeliner is a little sloppy, but otherwise, she looks great. She's a mom of two, spending a morning catching up with a friend at the park with her kids, not attending an awards show. Just because I care about what I wear doesn't mean I judge anyone else. Besides, it's not like I'm running a household and trying to wrangle two kids like Amber is.

I turn to give her my full attention and move my sunglasses to the top of my head. "You know that's not what I mean. What's wrong with you today? I always wear this kind of stuff."

She sighs. "I know. Sorry, I'm just being a bitch today. You just look so good all the time. I don't have time to put into my appearance anymore."

"Amber, my job involves working out all day. It's all I do! You need to be kinder to yourself. And you've been going to the gym. If you keep doing my courses—"

"I mean like my makeup and hair and clothes. I barely have time for anything anymore."

I can't hold back my sigh of frustration. I know she's grappling with self-confidence issues, and being around me doesn't help. But everything I say seems to only exacerbate the tension between us.

"I can only imagine how frustrating it must be to feel like you don't have time for yourself anymore," I tell her gently. "Look, why don't you talk to Anthony about taking the kids more often? So you can enjoy some you time?"

"Here we go," Amber mutters, rolling her eyes at me.

"I'm just saying, spending time away from the kids and reconnecting with who you are outside of motherhood is important. It might be just what you need to feel confident in yourself again."

She doesn't respond.

"You need to tell Anthony to watch the kids while you go out shopping or to the salon."

"You just don't get it, Sienna," she says harshly.

"What don't I get? You have the power to do something about it if you wanted."

She furrows her brows. "No I don't. My entire life centers around the boys. Something you wouldn't understand."

"You're not alone in parenting. Anthony can watch the boys. They're his kids, for God's sake," I say, not bothering to hide my anger. "You need to be honest with him and tell him he needs to step up as a parent."

"I don't expect you to understand. You only care about yourself."

I freeze, struggling to process the words that just came out of my best friend's mouth. "Excuse me?"

We've never fought like this. I don't know what triggered this argument. We've always supported each other, celebrated each other's victories.

"I didn't mean that," she says lamely. "Look, I'm just jealous that you get everything you want."

"No, I don't—"

"Really? Because that's not what it looks like from here. *Everything* works out for you."

"I get what I want because I go for what I want. I don't sit around and complain about my life," I snap back. Maybe that was harsh, but I'm over this.

"Why would I want to be like you? You don't even have a fucking car."

My anger reaches a boiling point. "At least my boyfriend isn't a man-child. You can't trust him to feed himself, let alone his kids."

Her eyes shoot daggers at me before she storms off towards the playground. "Come on, boys. We're going."

She walks them to her minivan—though not without a fight—and loads them in, pulling out of the parking lot without so much as a glance at me.

I watch them disappear from view, a knot forming in the pit of my stomach as I wrestle with the aftermath of our heated exchange. The silence that settles around me is as suffocating as the heat, heavy with the weight of our unresolved tension.

With tears blurring my vision, I call Liam. I can't believe Amber thinks I only care about myself. I love all my friends. I would do *anything* for Amber and the boys. The thought of our friendship falling apart breaks my heart.

Liam answers quickly. "What's going on?"

The sound of his voice brings me a small comfort despite the distance between us.

"Amber abandoned me at the park. We got into a huge fight, and she just left me here."

"Text me the address. I'll come get you."

"You don't have to leave work early. I can hang around here—"

"I'm already in my truck."

I smile to myself, despite the shitty afternoon. I text Liam the name of the park and look out at the empty swings, replaying the fight in my head. Maybe I instigated it. I suppose I was kind of bragging about Liam, and I know Amber's life is chaotic right now. Still, she could have at least pretended to be happy for me.

I sigh and shake my head. My mom taught me to be proud of what I've achieved, but I guess that pride gets in the way sometimes. Maybe that makes me seem egotistical and arrogant to others. I'll need to keep that in check around Liam; I don't want to start any fights with him.

Liam's black truck pulls into the parking lot, and I breathe a sigh of relief. My knight in shining armor hops out and jogs to me, wrapping his arms around me tightly. His immediate initiation of affection makes my heart flutter, and I snuggle into him. His presence is my safe haven, and I breathe him in.

"What happened?" he asks, concerned.

"I don't really know. She started acting all jealous about the way I look and how sweet you are. She implied that I was self-centered, and I called her boyfriend a man-child. She's overwhelmed with the kids, but she won't ask her boyfriend for help with them. I told her she needed to stop complaining about her life and do something about it."

He doesn't say anything; he just hugs me tighter. His silent support is exactly what I need. I'm glad he doesn't react or ask for more details. I don't think I could cope with any judgment from him.

He places a hand on my back and guides me into the truck. I wipe my tears away, determined to salvage the day as he hops into the driver's side. He remains quiet, as usual, and I let the silence stretch. I need to wrap my head around what happened before I can talk about it.

Eventually, we arrive at his place and walk inside. We'd planned on spending the weekend at the farm, but I hadn't packed a bag yet.

I step out the back door to get some comfort from Zoe. She would never call me self-centered or make fun of me for not having a car.

She runs up to me with her tail wagging, and I wrap her in a hug.

Liam joins me, and we pet Zoe until she gets tired of us and heads down the steps into the yard.

"Do you want to talk about it?" he asks quietly.

"I don't know what happened. I was just talking about how great you are, but instead of being happy that I'd finally found someone I like, she didn't care at all. She scowled at me like I'd spit in her cereal." I lean back and gaze up at the sky. "She said I get everything I want. That I don't care about anyone but myself. I don't know where that came from."

He nods in understanding, but he doesn't say anything.

"Let's just forget about it," I say, trying to let the events of the afternoon wash away. "We should take Zoe to the farm with us."

Liam shakes his head. "She drools in the car."

"That's not her fault. Come on, she'd love it there! And you said you want to give her more space."

He seems to think it over. After a moment of silence, he lets out a resigned sigh.

"Fine."

Chapter 23
Liam

I spend Friday evening wiping Zoe's drool from my truck's back seat. It's unnerving how quickly I gave in to Sienna, and I wonder how much I would do just to see her smile.

I wake early on Saturday morning and decide to cut the grass, leaving Sienna sleeping peacefully in my childhood bed again. She needs to rest after her emotional day with Amber. I don't know the background of their relationship well enough to fully understand what happened, but it's clear that Amber's comments have shaken her. I'm not sure I would be willing to stay friends with someone who called me 'self-centered', but Sienna's not nearly as ruthless as I am. No doubt she'll forgive Amber soon enough. I just hope whatever bitterness or jealousy Amber is feeling doesn't rear its head again.

After finishing the grass, checking and repairing the fences, tidying up the barn, and fixing the railing on the dock, I head to the backyard to find Sienna and Zoe running through the grass, playing. As the sun rises higher in the sky, casting golden rays across the farm, I take a moment to admire the picturesque scene. The vibrant hues of green and the gentle rustling of leaves in the breeze create a tranquil atmosphere—a stark contrast to the frenetic energy of Sienna and Zoe.

"I don't know who has more energy, you or Zoe," I call out. "Did you take her for a walk earlier?"

"Of course! We walked four miles, didn't we, girl?" she answers, nuzzling her face against Zoe's.

She's not winded or tired in the slightest, and I shake my head in disbelief. The sounds of chirping birds and buzzing insects mingle with the distant lowing of cattle, creating a symphony of nature that soothes my soul.

I find a ball and start playing fetch with Zoe, her energy never wavering. She's a black-and-white blur over the grass, and I relish the fun I'm having with both of my girls here.

My girls. The thought warms my chest; thinking of Sienna as mine is far too satisfying. I know this thing between us is evolving every day, but we haven't officially labeled our relationship yet. I shouldn't feel this possessive so early on.

Sienna flips around the yard, doing various cartwheels and back handsprings. Of course she knows how to do that stuff. She smiles all the while, having the time of her life out here with me.

As I watch Sienna's graceful movements, I'm struck by the realization that she embodies the spirit of the farm itself—wild, untamed, and utterly captivating. Her exuberance reminds me to embrace the present moment and find joy in the simple pleasures.

Everything she does, she does for herself, not to show off for others. When she danced with her friends at the bar, she was dancing simply to have fun. It wasn't performative.

And now, she's doing gymnastics in my backyard, not to impress me, but simply because it's fun. She dresses for herself, works out for herself... I can't help but admire her self-assurance, her sheer delight at simply being alive.

When I'm with her, I'm liberated, as if the constraints of

everyday life have been lifted from my shoulders. With her by my side, life is full of endless possibilities.

I've never felt more alive than in these past few weeks, and I don't want to hold back any longer. I walk over to her, unable to stop myself, like a planet succumbing to the sun's gravitational pull.

Cupping her face, I lean in and kiss her.

Her hands grip my thighs as she kisses me back, the feel of her mouth on mine sending pure elation washing over me.

The farm has always been my happy place, but with her here, it's paradise.

I pull back, and she sways with dizziness. I grab her arms to steady her, but my smugness fades as I realize it wasn't the kiss that made her dizzy but the flipping she was just doing.

I let go of her arms, not sure what to say. She looks up at me, concern in her gaze as she recognizes the panic in my eyes.

"Shi— sorry, I shouldn't— Let's just forget that happened."

I walk away before I can see her reaction.

By some miracle, Sienna hasn't taken my car and driven off into the sunset after my slip-up. I expected her to confront me or storm off in frustration at my insistence on taking things slow when I clearly can't control my desire for her. Instead, she seems to take the dismissal of our kiss in stride, and we're able to enjoy a pleasant evening. I cook her dinner, pasta this time, and we watch a few movies before falling asleep on the couch, Sienna's head nestled against my chest.

We don't address the kiss or our relationship, and I'm

grateful for Sienna's seemingly endless patience with me.

We head back to my house early Sunday morning so I can go to church with my parents. Sienna stayed there after I explained that I wasn't ready for her to meet my family yet. She took that in stride as well. That wasn't the only reason she couldn't come with me to church. The only clothes she had were a nude, form-fitting top that showed off a lot of cleavage and shorts and sandals.

She didn't seem to mind hanging around my house with Zoe, who is slowly becoming an inside dog. I left her with a huge plate of strawberry and banana French toast, and she was happy as a clam.

As I sit beside my parents in church, my mind flicks through my memories of the past few weeks. Sienna has never pressured me to talk about my feelings, to define our relationship, or to open up about how I feel about her. I asked her to be patient with me, and that's exactly what she's done. Despite me unintentionally giving her mixed signals, which have undoubtedly been confusing as hell, she's been compassionate, gentle, forgiving, and honest with me.

It's more than I could ever have asked for. I can't deny the peace she brings into my life. I had no idea when she messaged me that things would work out this way, but I couldn't be happier.

As we exit the church, Mom turns to me.

"It seems like you're doing better."

I nod and look away. I'm not ready to tell my family about Sienna yet, but I also don't want to lie. "It's getting easier."

"Good," she replies, smiling. "You know, the Robertsons' daughter is single again. Maybe you should reach out to her."

I shake my head. "I'm good."

"That's a shame. She's really cute."

"I guess."

She eyes me skeptically, and I give her a quick hug.

"See you next Sunday," I tell her before rushing off to get back home to Sienna.

I can't see her as I walk through the front door, so I assume she's outside with Zoe. I change into more comfortable clothes—gray sweatpants and a black T-shirt—before going to look for her.

I spot her blonde hair on the back porch.

Sliding the door open, I take a seat in the chair next to hers.

"How was church?" she asks, giving me a once-over that slows down at my crotch.

My body instantly responds, and I find myself spreading my legs and leaning back in the chair, causing our knees to touch slightly. "Fine."

She pulls her hair off her neck in a makeshift ponytail, and I can't fight the image of my own hands pulling her hair back instead. I don't bother looking away. I know she wants me to appreciate her body.

"Oh my gosh," she breathes, fanning herself. "It's hot out today."

I don't know if she's purposefully trying to tempt me or if being sexy just comes naturally to her. The tan-colored top she's wearing makes her look practically naked, and it's padded in a way that pushes her boobs up. I don't bother to pretend I'm not looking at her tits.

She opens her mouth to say something, but I'm denied the pleasure of another sexy comment. Her eyes go wide as she hears a silly jingle coming from down the road.

"Is that an actual ice cream truck?" She jumps up from her chair. "I haven't had a firecracker popsicle in years!"

She leaves me on the porch like chopped liver as she rushes through the house, presumably to wait on the street with cash in hand.

I shake my head and enjoy the tranquility of the backyard while she's gone, until she eventually returns with a red, white, and blue popsicle on a stick.

Plopping back down in her chair, she raises it to her mouth.

"Mmm," she moans at the taste. She throws her head back and closes her eyes. "That's so good."

She wraps her lips around the top of the popsicle and sucks, her cheeks hollowing slightly. She pulls it away and licks her lips seductively. I can't tell if she's genuinely enjoying the taste or if this is for my sake.

Either way, I can't tear my gaze away as she moves her head up and down the popsicle, keeping her hand still. She licks up the side of it slowly.

Oh yeah, this is for me. But I don't give a fuck if it's performative. It's a damn good performance.

I'm mesmerized as she continues to suck and lick the popsicle. The suggestive nature of the act and the sound of her mouth sliding up and down the ice-cold treat has my cock hardening beneath my sweatpants, which I'm sure is exactly what she wants.

The sound of her sucking turns me on, and I stare straight at her as she savors the cool sweetness on her tongue. If she wants to play, then fuck it. I'm game.

Her eyes drift shut in bliss as she indulges in the icy treat, her cheeks turning pink. With deliberate slowness, she traces her tongue along the length of the popsicle, gazing straight into my eyes as her lips glisten with red juice. Soft, breathy sounds escape her parted lips, and the eroticism of it makes me want to shove her on her knees in front of me.

Her teasing smile dissolves any doubt about her intention, and I slowly reach out to wrap my hand around hers. We grip the stick of the popsicle together, and I slowly pull her to stand between my legs.

She lowers herself to her knees in front of me, melting rivulets of sweetness trickling down the popsicle stick onto my hand. The same red juice traces the contours of her lips and chin, the sight making me fully hard.

She bobs her head up and down the popsicle, gagging as it touches the back of her throat. The sound of her choking on it goes straight to my cock. Her graceful and fluid movements give me a glimpse into what I could have if she was my girlfriend.

She sucks and swallows the popsicle loudly, and I swear I could finish from just the sight of her between my legs. She lifts her head with a mischievous grin once nothing remains but the stick, and I toss it aside. She remains between my legs, looking up at me with glistening lips. I'm completely entranced, thinking with the wrong head, as I wrap my hand around the back of her head.

I move to lower my sweatpants, and she doesn't stop me. I lower them to my knees, and she slowly runs her hands up my thighs. She rubs the outline of my dick through my underwear as I run my fingers through her silky strands. She pulls my cock out from my underwear, eyes widening as she takes in the sight. The smug smile on her face tells me she likes what she sees. She wraps a manicured hand around my length and opens her mouth.

"That's it, angel," I praise. Her tongue gets closer and closer to the underside of my cock, but before she can lick it, we're interrupted by a knock on the front door.

She stops in her tracks, and I want to murder whoever is standing on the other side of the door.

"Just ignore it," I command, my eyes pleading with her to continue. I've never been this desperate for release, and I'm moments away from begging her to suck my dick.

Before she makes another move, the front door opens, and two sets of footsteps sound through the house.

"Liam!" my brother calls out.

I let out a frustrated breath and throw my head back. I'm shoving my dick back into my pants as the back door slides open.

Sienna quickly rises from her knees, but we're too late. My brother's mouth opens like a fish, his eyes as big as saucers. Riley stands behind him, covering her face.

"Well, hello there," Nathan exclaims, beaming. "I'm Nathan. I'd shake your hand but uh..."

I stand up awkwardly. "This is Sienna."

She waves cutely. He should be getting a slap across the face for interrupting us.

"Sienna," he repeats approvingly, eyeing her up and down. "I'm Liam's brother, and this is my girlfriend, Riley."

"Nice to meet you," Sienna says softly, blushing bright red.

Seeing her flustered is a rare sight.

Nathan shoots me a proud look, more proud than he was on my graduation day or the day I landed my job. He's grinning like an idiot. I just scowl at him, trying to figure out the fastest way to get them out of my house.

"We brought you a case of beer to cheer you up, but I see that *job* has already been taken care of," my brother jokes.

I roll my eyes, but his teasing causes a deep blush to creep up Sienna's neck. "Let's go inside," I suggest to nudge them towards the front door.

I feel the need to defend Sienna, but I don't know how. I can't say that wasn't what we were doing because it's exactly what it looked like. Her tongue was centimeters from my dick—thank God they didn't see that.

"We were gonna see if you wanted to get lunch," Riley says.

"Babe," Nathan interjects, "I think they have plans."

"We weren't— That wasn't... what it looked like," Sienna stammers.

Despite everything, a part of me is enjoying seeing Sienna blush and trip over her words. She's always so self-assured. I wasn't sure she was even capable of feeling embarrassed. I lean back on the counter and enjoy the show.

She looks to me for help, but I don't give her anything. Her eyes plead for me to jump in, but I'm not sure what to say. Nathan and Riley know exactly what we were doing. Trying to come up with a cover story would be pointless. Besides, I prefer to let the chips fall where they may, and I'm having way too much fun seeing Sienna tongue-tied.

"Do you want us to leave?" Nathan asks.

YES.

"No, don't be silly, you don't have to go," Sienna offers.

Fuck.

Sienna turns to me. "Let's all get lunch," she suggests,

watching for my reaction.

"Great!" Nathan replies, looking at me smugly. "We can get to know your..."

Sienna looks at me expectantly. I know what she wants me to say. Girlfriend. Is that what she is now? I falter, wishing we could take a moment to talk about what almost happened.

"Friend," I finally answer.

Sienna casts her eyes downwards, only for a second, but I notice all the same. I hate disappointing her, hate the thought of her not knowing how much I want her to be mine. But we need to at least talk things through before we enter into an official relationship.

We decide on the local bar and grill, so Sienna and I hop into my truck and I pull out of the driveway. The normally comfortable silence between us is now charged with tension.

I scramble for words, unsure how to explain that I want her in my life, that I have strong feelings for her, that I've never connected with someone this much.

"Should we talk about what almost happened?" I finally say.

"What's there to talk about? We got carried away."

"Yeah, but—"

"Let's just forget it happened."

I swallow tightly. I didn't expect having my own words thrown back at me to cut so deep.

Chapter 24
Sienna

As we step into the bar and grill, the scent of sizzling burgers and the hum of lively chatter fill the air, providing a welcome distraction from the awkwardness. The four of us slide into a cozy booth, the tension between me and Liam at an all-time high. We sit close enough that our arms brush against each other, yet there's an invisible barrier that separates us.

My shoulders tense, and I avoid looking at Nathan and Riley. Meeting Liam's brother and his girlfriend like this is not how I envisioned it. I don't want them to get the wrong idea about me.

Silence hangs between us, which I should be grateful for. I don't want to make this lunch any more uncomfortable than it is by trying to explain what was going on. I'm still flustered and embarrassed, and I glance up at Liam for help. He doesn't spare me a look as we peruse the menus, his expression guarded and stoic as usual.

Do I wish he had introduced me as his girlfriend? Yes. But I promised I'd be patient with him, and that's exactly what I'll continue to do. His guarded heart is one of the things I love about him. He's sweet and sensitive underneath the tough guy exterior.

I put my menu down and place a gentle hand on his leg. He looks at me, and I try to reassure him with my eyes, seeking the same from him in return. We lock gazes, and he gives me a subtle smile, covering my hand with his and squeezing. I breathe a soft sigh of relief. We're going to be okay. We'll figure this out.

I take his hand in mine, interlocking our fingers, and we look across the table at Nathan and Riley, who watch us with unabashed curiosity. They stare openly at us, as if surprised by what they saw.

Before they can say anything, the waiter arrives to take our orders.

Once he leaves, Nathan and Riley bombard us with questions.

"Where'd you guys meet?" Riley asks.

Her light brown hair complements her hazel eyes, which are a couple of shades lighter than my own.

I fidget with my nails, unsure how to answer. There's no way I can tell the truth: that I treated LinkedIn like my own personal dating pool, refining a list of attractive men with high-paying salaries until Liam's profile caught my eye.

"Instagram," I say simply, hoping that will be enough. It's sort of the truth. That is where we met digitally. "We messaged each other before meeting up for coffee a few weeks ago."

"So, who messaged who first?" Nathan asks. His sandy blonde hair differs from Liam's dark brown locks, but his identical brown eyes give way to a strong resemblance to his brother.

"I did," I answer.

Riley furrows her brow at my response.

"Cool, cool," Nathan continues. "So, what do you do?"

"I'm a Pilates instructor."

He turns his face up to the ceiling, a massive grin on his face, as if he's proud of his brother for landing a girl like me.

He recovers and looks back down, still beaming with pride. "Is that pretty lucrative?"

Riley looks at him disapprovingly, but I don't mind the question.

"Not really," I tell him. "Let's just say I live modestly."

Riley presses her lips together in a tight line, but she keeps her opinion to herself.

"What about you guys?" I ask.

"We're in college," Nathan answers. "I'm undeclared, but Riley's going to law school."

"Yup," she says. "I don't want to rely on someone else to support me financially. I prefer to earn my own keep by working hard and earning what I have."

Ah, so that's what this is about.

"That's smart. A woman's gotta have financial independence."

She eyes me skeptically, but before I can say anything, the waiter returns with our food. He sets a bacon cheeseburger, a double side of fries, and a root beer float in front of me.

I realize Liam hasn't said a word since we sat down. He digs into his meal—steak and mashed potatoes—keeping to himself.

"How's your steak?" I ask him.

"Fine."

I'm used to his curt answers by now, so I don't push.

We eat in silence for a while before Nathan pipes up again. "I'm surprised a Pilates instructor would order all that."

"That's the best part about my job. It keeps me in shape so

I can eat whatever I want. Every day is a cheat day."

"I wish I had abs, but I can't do all those exercises," Riley says, shaking her head. "I tried an ab workout once. I was sore for a week!"

"It's all about baby steps," I tell her. "You should start with a beginner's course. I teach one every Monday, Wednesday, Friday."

She nods. "I'll try it."

"I'll text you the name of the gym. You can do the class for free, and we can walk the track afterward."

Riley nods. "Sounds great, let's do it. We should get to know each other if you're going to be hanging around."

"I plan to," I tell her, looking at Liam and smiling.

It's clear I have Nathan's approval, but Riley will take some time to win over. I'm not worried. She'll come around in no time.

We wave goodbye to Nathan and Riley outside the bar and grill, driving back to the house in silence.

As the front door clicks shut behind us, Liam turns, caging me against the wall.

"You think you can tease me like that?" he says low in my ear.

His throaty voice goes straight to my pussy, and I'm reminded of how damp my panties got during my popsicle faux blow job. My heart races in my chest. I thought for sure Liam would be all awkward and keep a polite distance when we got back from lunch, but my performance on the back deck clearly had more of an effect on him than I thought.

"Are you jealous of a popsicle?" I tease.

His sly smile promises things that threaten to make my legs shake with need. "I have more to offer than that popsicle. But you know that."

Yes, I do. My mouth had watered at the sight of his cock: long, rock hard, and all for me.

I place my hands on his chest, running them over the fabric of his t-shirt. "Hmm, but do you taste as good?"

"Oh, angel." He lets out a throaty chuckle. "You have no idea what you've started."

He captures my lips with his own, trailing the backs of his fingers down the side of my neck. "Do you want to finish what you started?"

"What *I* started? You totally came on to me."

He pulls back. "You think *I* came on to *you*?" he says in utter disbelief. He backs away from me without taking his eyes off mine.

I smile at getting such a reaction from him. That's not easy to do. "Uh, yeah," I say as if it should be obvious. "Come on, the gray sweatpants. Brushing your knee against mine. Staring at my tits. You were eye-fucking me out there."

He stammers, "You... I..."

I giggle, reveling in his rare loss for words. I love the effect I have on him.

I cock my head innocently. "Care to finish what you started?"

He cups my face, pressing his lips to mine and pinning my body against the wall with his. The feel of his hardening cock against my core makes me gasp, and as I part my lips, he plunges his tongue into my mouth. His rough hand on the side of my throat makes me crave them all over my body, caressing every inch of my skin.

He lifts me by the waist, and I wrap my legs around him. He wears me like a belt all the way to his bedroom. Laying me down on the king-sized bed, he steps back for a moment, ripping his shirt off and tossing it to the side. In one swift move, he removes his sweatpants, leaving him standing before me, wearing nothing but tight black briefs and black crew socks. I lick my lips as I trace the lines of his lean body, his dick imprint, his hard muscles.

He grips my hips and drags me to the edge of the bed so that the corner of the mattress is between my legs. I remove my top at the same time he removes my shorts and panties in one quick move. Reaching around to unhook my bra, I drop it to the ground, letting Liam's eyes devour my naked body.

He stares in awe, in reverence, before he places one hand on my waist, gripping tightly. His calloused hands travel up to my breast, and he paws it roughly before sticking his thumb between my lips.

I open my mouth wide, inviting his touch, and he rubs the pad of his thumb over my tongue, massaging it as I stick it out. The playfulness of the gesture makes me smile, and he returns my smile with his own, bending down to trace hot, wet kisses over my sensitive skin.

Gone is my quiet, shy, guarded Liam. Confident, self-assured Liam has taken his place, and I can't say that I hate this new side of him.

The wet sounds of our kisses fill the dimly lit room, turning me on as much as his hands roaming over my body, brushing my hair over my shoulder. He gropes my other breast before backing away again, his intense gaze appreciating the sight of my naked body on his bed.

I'm so turned on, I can't think straight, and I subconsciously ride the corner of his mattress, desperate for his touch, but he's making me wait. Or maybe he's trying to savor the moment.

He steps closer, tenderly rubbing his hand over my stomach, his large hand covering it at the smallest part. His hand travels further up to massage one of my tits, his thumb rubbing over the nipple.

I continue riding the corner of the mattress as he climbs onto the bed next to me, his knees making an indent in the mattress. Pulling his briefs down, he frees his cock, inches away from my face.

Finishing what I started on the back deck, I tenderly lift it into my mouth and suck on the head. I turn onto my side for a better angle and continue bobbing my head back and forth.

"God, you're beautiful," he whispers as I moan around his length. "You're perfect."

Enjoying the praise, I nuzzle into him, taking his cock further down my throat.

"Oh, angel," he moans.

His fingers find my clit, rubbing in teasing circles as his other hand cradles the back of my head. As I suck his velvety soft dick, he reaches his hand around the back of my head and pulls my hair back from my face. I can't get enough of his groans of pleasure.

Pulling back, I look up playfully, my mouth open and spit resting on my tongue. He rubs his thumb over my tongue and bottom lip, spreading the saliva around and gazing down at me in absolute admiration.

The pride in his eyes makes me want to satisfy him, and I take his cock back into my mouth, deep-throating and gagging as I touch my nose to his stomach. He lets out a soft cry of pleasure, and I pull back with a smile. A string of saliva connects my mouth and his cock, and I giggle and twirl the strand with my finger.

He steps off the bed and removes his underwear, giving me the chance to back up on the bed and settle in the middle, watching his lean body climb over me. I expect him to kiss me, but his face stops at my pussy.

Diving in with no hesitation, his lips capture my clit, his tongue circling with an intensity that has me bowing off the bed.

I can't control the sounds coming out of my mouth as he spreads my pussy open with his fingers and presses his face in further. I bounce my body as he nods his head up and down, breathing heavily as he draws me closer to the edge. His tongue plunges deep inside, and I grip the hair on the back of his head.

"Oh, *fuck*," I moan. His tongue rubbing my clit takes me to the edge, and I scream out in pleasure.

I breathe heavily and let out a playful giggle as he continues to lap up my arousal. Riding his face greedily, I'm in awe of the way he went for it, head-on—no pun intended.

This can't be the same man I've spent weeks getting to know. This version of Liam is assertive, handsy, and bold.

Rising from between my legs, Liam gives me a smug grin, bringing the tip of his cock to my center. He towers over me on his knees, his hard muscles making him look seductive and powerful.

He grips his cock and rests it over my pelvis, the head reaching my belly button. He teases me with it before plunging it inside me.

He pauses halfway at my groan of pleasure and pain, allowing me to adjust before continuing, slowly pushing his cock all the way to the hilt. He stops again as I pant beneath him, circling my clit with his thumb. My body slowly relaxes, and I give him a nod, encouraging him to withdraw before plunging back inside. He keeps his pace steady until he begins to pump in and out without holding back.

Gripping my waist tightly, he thrusts fiercely.

I toss my head back in pleasure, moaning as he fucks me over and over, his thumb maintaining a constant pressure on my clit. I lift my head to watch him fuck me, and the hard muscles of his abs contract as he hits a spot inside me that none of my previous partners have been able to reach. He's the epitome of sexiness, with his long cock and tight abs. His thumbs dig into my belly, and he uses me for leverage as he thrusts into me.

His breathing becomes heavier, his eyes glistening with fevered desperation as he rubs my clit, hard. I feel my walls clenching around him as I come apart, and he groans as he falls on top of me. He wraps his arms around me tightly and uses my body for his own pleasure as he finishes inside me.

"Fuck, baby," he mutters, running his hands gently over my face before rolling onto his back.

Beaming with satisfaction, I snuggle up next to him, both of us completely naked except for his black crew socks.

I feel dirty, used, fucked. I love it.

Liam fell asleep within seconds, as if he gave it his all before collapsing onto the bed. I use the time to admire his tall, slender, muscular physique. Black crew socks cover his feet and ankles, and his calves and thighs are solid muscle.

His dick appears a bit smaller than before—I guess he's a grower—but still impressive. The pubic region is covered with small, black, curly hairs surrounding his pelvis, lower stomach, and upper thighs. The sheer masculinity of his body has me wet all over again.

The hard muscles of his abs entice me, and I drag a finger over them. My abs come from the gym, but his come from hard work and manual labor. They aren't for show, unlike the guys I see in the gym all the time who build their bodies for vanity.

I rest back down on the bed and think about everything that's happened over the last few days.

I broke one of my cardinal rules: never have sex with a man who doesn't want a relationship, and though Liam's been giving me mixed signals on that front, I'm fairly confident he's just worried about rushing into something unless he's sure. I can understand that—I'm usually the same, after all. There's just something about our chemistry that makes us both lose control around each other.

Liam does want a relationship with me; he's just not ready yet. Or maybe that's just what I'm telling myself.

The night after the bar, he told me he wanted to be with me, but he didn't want to jump into a new relationship. So the real question is, do I believe him?

He says he can't stay away from me, but what if that was just a line to get me into bed? I've never had so many doubts, and I'm not sure where to go from here.

I've never been one to sit around and wallow in self-pity, and I'm not gonna start now. I gently ease out of bed and head for the shower. The harsh fluorescent light of the bathroom reveals twin bruises blemishing my stomach. There's no doubt he left a lasting impression, both mentally and physically.

As if a switch was flipped, Liam became rough and demanding, creating a mix of pain and pleasure inside me. I've never had sex like that—unrestrained passion and raw, primal energy.

I step into the small corner shower and let the hot water run over me. The water pressure is impressive, practically creating indents on my scalp, and I savor the feeling of finally getting clean.

I've been wearing the same clothes all weekend, and the various activities of the past couple of days have taken a toll on my hygiene. I stand under the water and let it wash away the dirt and sweat from my nature walk at the farm, the leftover stickiness from the popsicle on my chest, and the stickiness between my legs from my filthy endeavors on the bed right outside this bathroom.

The hot water feels too good to leave, and I stay long enough that the water turns cold. Begrudgingly, I turn the water off and grab a towel. I don't hear anything, so I assume Liam is still sleeping.

As I step out of the bathroom wearing only a towel, Liam walks into the bedroom with an armful of snacks and drinks. I drop the towel and help him set the items on the dresser—a mixture of sweet and salty snacks.

"What's all this for?"

"We're not leaving this room for a while."

Chapter 25
Liam

I wrap my arms around Sienna and hold her close as the evening sun streams through the window. The warmth of her body and the sun create an atmosphere of comfort and intimacy in my bedroom, a stark contrast to the cold loneliness that plagued the space just weeks ago.

"You are so perfect," I whisper, pressing a gentle kiss to her ear before moving to kiss her cheek. "Incredible." I kiss her jaw. "Flawless."

My fingers glide through her soft, messy hair as I murmur words of love and appreciation. She breathes deeply as I softly stroke her back, and her smile is one of pure comfort and relaxation.

She shifts slightly, revealing two bruises on her stomach.

"Oh, angel. Are those from me?" I ask softly, bringing my lips to them to place gentle kisses where my thumbs dug in during our first time.

She nods shyly.

"Turn over. Let me take care of you."

She rolls onto her stomach, giving me a full view of her toned backside. I run my hands down her back and up again, applying gentle pressure, soothing her muscles. Her body relaxes under my touch, and I have to restrain myself from sliding my fingers inside her again. She's exhausted from the physical exertion, so I rub her shoulders instead.

Once her body is well and truly sinking into the mattress, I lie back down next to her, placing soft kisses against her cheek until she lifts her head up to meet my mouth with hers. It's a slow, languorous kiss—perfect for a lazy weekend.

"Don't you want to shower?" she asks softly. "I kind of... came all over your face."

"I want to make sure you're taken care of."

She smiles wistfully, resting her head on my chest. I don't have the words to tell her how much she means to me, but I can be present and attentive to her. I want to comfort and reassure her about my feelings, but I also don't want to say the wrong thing and mess up what we have.

For now, my actions will just have to speak for me.

"*As the sun dipped low on the horizon, casting a golden glow over the rugged landscape, Jake felt his heart stir with a wild longing,*" I read aloud from the paperback.

Sienna lies with her head on my lap, the soft evening light filtering through the windows of her living room. The heavenly scent of one of her candles adds to the cozy atmosphere.

I came here straight after work. I meant it when I said I couldn't stay away. Now she's got me reading one of those old novels I bought her.

"*His eyes met hers across the dusty corral, and in that moment, he knew he'd found his home in the depths of her soul.*"

Sienna giggles, and I have to still her fidgeting legs with my hand as I try to focus on the words. The sight of my palm gripping her thigh distracts me from my reading. The little minx just smiles at me, hiding her grin behind her hands. She's changed from her workout attire into a matching sweatshirt and shorts set, and she looks as adorable as ever.

"*With a gentle hand, he brushed a stray lock of hair from her windswept face, his touch igniting a spark that set their hearts ablaze,*" I read dramatically. "*Beneath the vast expanse of the endless sky, they stood, two souls entwined in a love as timeless as the rolling plains themselves. For in each other's arms, they found a refuge from the storms of life, a haven where their love could bloom like the wildflowers in springtime.*"

I close the book, rolling my eyes. "You actually enjoyed that?"

Sienna's laughter bubbles up again. "Oh, I loved it. The romance, the passion, the *heat*," she gushes. "And I loved it more when you read it." Her eyes sparkle with amusement as she glances up at me, her gaze filled with playful teasing. "Your voice is so seductive, you could narrate audiobooks for a living."

I shake my head, though her compliment makes my stomach flutter. It's almost pathetic how desperate I am for her to like every part of me. "This is what gets you going?"

"I can't help it! It's so erotic and sensual. I like 'em spicy," she says, her voice a delightful melody that lifts my spirits after a long day at work.

"You realize this is secondhand, right?" I tease. "Have you ever considered how many other women have 'got themselves going' when reading it?"

"Eww... why did you have to say that?" She sits up on the couch.

"I need to go wash my hands," I joke, setting the book down on the coffee table.

As I head to the kitchen, Sienna follows me.

"What candle do you have going today?" I ask her, drying my hands with a towel.

"Coconut Cream Pie."

I smile to myself as I start taking out the ingredients we bought for dinner. The anticipation of cooking together fills me with a sense of excitement. I can't wait for her to try my food again.

She catches my lips tilting up at the corners. "What are you smiling about?"

I look her up and down. She radiates warmth and charm in her cozy cream-colored sweatshirt and shorts.

"That's what you smelled like when we first met at the coffee shop," I recall fondly. "Coconut Cream Pie."

"You were smelling me?"

I take the ground beef out of the fridge and dump it into a frying pan. "Not on purpose."

She heads into her room while I brown the meat on the stove. When Sienna comes back out, she stands next to me. It takes a second, but I smell that delightful scent again coming from her skin.

I nuzzle into her neck and breathe in the sweet fragrance. "That's the one."

She giggles as my beard tickles her skin, pressing her hands into my chest. She playfully pushes me away and hops onto the counter.

"I like to smell good," she says, dangling her tan legs. "That's why I couldn't wait to get back home and shower with my own stuff. I can't believe how dirty I got over the weekend."

I step in between her legs, murmuring in her ear, "Oh, I remember. My room *also* smelled like cream pie."

"Liam!" She laughs.

I smirk as she pushes me away again. "I had to wash my sheets, but there was something on the corner that was a little... harder to get out... You don't happen to know anything about that, do you?"

She blushes furiously, her cheeks practically on fire. "I don't know what came over me," she says shyly, shaking her head.

"I do," I say with a wink.

I've discovered over the weekend that Sienna's self-assurance tends to waver when it comes to talking directly about sex. She's full of unabashed confidence most of the time, but when it comes to talking about her own sexual pleasure, she gets all shy.

Returning my focus to the stove, I contemplate how easy it's been to be playful and mischievous with Sienna. I was never this comfortable teasing any of my exes like this. I also never talked about sex so openly. It's refreshing, but that anxious part of me wonders whether what I've found with Sienna is just too good to be true.

"Can I help?"

Sienna's question brings me back to the present. "Sure. You can put the buns in the oven."

She stops moving, staring off into space. Her face drops, and I realize the double entendre.

Shit. We haven't talked about any of that. Sienna seemed to have no problem with us having sex without a condom, so I can only assume she's on the pill. I know I'm clean, too, so there's no risk there... at least on my part. My thoughts are spiraling, but I can't seem to get any words out.

The awkward tension hangs in the air, casting a shadow over the moment.

"For the... sliders," I eventually say, deciding to save the 'safe sex' conversation for later.

"Right," she says, hopping off the counter. She grabs a pack of Hawaiian rolls and takes them out of the package, setting them on the pan. "I'm not much of a cook," she admits.

"I'll show you." I grab a knife and wrap my arms around her to show her how to cut them all in half at the same time. I shamelessly sniff her hair, eliciting another giggle from her. The playfulness of the moment helps us both relax, and just like that, we've returned to our easy comfort with each other.

I spread the meat over the bottom halves of the rolls, and she follows behind with sliced cheese. I replace the top halves, and she moves to put the pan in the oven.

"Wait, there's one more step." I open the fridge. "This right here will step up your burger game."

I pull out a tub of butter and spoon some into a bowl.

I heat the bowl in the microwave before brushing the butter over the buns.

"Mmm, they smell so good," Sienna hums, placing the tray carefully in the oven before closing the door. "Do you want something to drink while we wait?" she asks.

"Sure."

She whips up two rum and cokes, and as I sip mine, I'm more aware than ever that we are avoiding important topics. We haven't talked about her and her friend's fight, how my brother caught us on the back porch, what sex means for our relationship, birth control—nothing.

"Sit down," I tell her. "I'll take care of the rest."

I set the table with plates and our drinks, along with a bowl of creamy burger sauce to dip the sliders in. Once the cheese is melted, I take the pan out of the oven and bring it to the table. The smell of sizzling meat makes my mouth water, and we eagerly dig in.

Sienna pulls off a slider dripping with butter and cheese and dips it into the sauce. I watch expectantly as she lifts it to her mouth. Her eyes roll to the back of her head as she takes the first bite.

"Oh my God, this is amazing."

"I'll take that eye roll as a five-star review."

"Ten stars. Twenty stars. A million!" she says, shoving the rest into her mouth.

I can't help but smile. "That's the reaction I aim for every time."

Satisfaction and pride course through me at her enjoyment, and I take a sip of my rum and coke, the sweetness contrasting with the saltiness of the burgers.

"Your drinks are delicious."

"Thanks. Just remember not to drink them too quickly," she teases. "On second thought, drink as much as you want."

"Oh, I won't be doing that again. I don't know how you make such strong drinks that don't even taste like alcohol."

"It's a gift," she says smugly.

We finish our meals, and she lets me sit while she takes care of cleanup. As she wipes the counter, I notice her itching her chest. She comes to stand next to me at the table, and I stand and lower her sweatshirt to see that her chest is red and splotchy.

"What happened?"

"Oh, it's this necklace," she explains, lifting the dainty gold chain and teardrop diamond—the same necklace she wore to the cafe. "It's pretty, but cheap. It breaks me out every time I wear it." She takes it off and drops it into the trashcan.

For some reason, I feel insulted. I don't want my girl wearing cheap jewelry.

Sienna makes two more rum and cokes, and we sit back down on the couch.

"We can watch that show of yours again. If you want."

"Are you sure? We can watch something else," Sienna offers, pulling a blanket over our legs.

I wrap my arm around her and pull her into my side, wanting to be close to her. "No, it's fine. We can watch it."

She gives me a knowing smile. "You want to know who A is, don't you?"

"Yes," I admit. "And I want to find out if that teacher goes to jail."

Chapter 26
Sienna

VERONICA

Help help help

ME

What's going on?

VERONICA

Walking home from work. Creepy guy wouldn't
leave his booth for hours.

ME

Is he following you?

VERONICA

Maybe.

ME

Act normal. Call me and stay on the phone until
you get home.

"Hey, girl," V says, a slight shake in her voice.

"Hey, V, how was work?" I ask, holding the phone to my
ear. The sounds of the busy street filter through the receiver.

"Oh, you know. The usual. Taking orders and bringing
food to people," she replies, tension underlying her casual tone.

"Where are you now?"

"Walking down Church Street. I'm almost to that bakery where we bought the key lime cheesecake we had for Chloe's birthday."

"Ooh, I remember that day," I say with a chuckle, trying to put her at ease. "Her dog jumped up all excited and pulled her dress down, and she flashed her entire family."

"The dangers of off-the-shoulder dresses," V jokes weakly. "I feel kinda bad. She borrowed that dress from me."

"Is that why it barely covered her underwear?"

"Hey, she pulled it off."

"Yeah, so did Dexter," I say, getting a laugh from her.

"Okay, I'm almost home."

"Do you want me to come over?" I ask, worried. She knows I'd be there in a heartbeat.

"No, you don't have to. I'm walking up the front steps now." Her voice carries a note of relief.

I hear the door open and close.

"All right. I'm home and safe inside. Thanks for—" She stops abruptly.

"V? What's going on?" My heart races.

"Someone's knocking on the door."

Loud thumps on her door sound through the phone.

"That wasn't knocking; that was banging," I argue, my own anxiety mounting.

"Should I answer it?"

"Hell no! Just stay there. I'm on my way."

"I promise I'm fine," she assures me, but I'm already out the door.

She gasps. "He's jiggling the knob."

Adrenaline surges through me as I rush down the street,

weaving through pedestrians. Thank God I'm already in workout gear and sneakers.

"I'll be there as fast as I can. Do not open the door."

Ten minutes later, I sprint up the steps to V's apartment. She opens the door quickly, her eyes darting anxiously to the street.

"I guess he left," she says, her voice shaky. "Are you okay?"

I step into her apartment. "Me? Yeah, why?" I pant, bending over with my hands on my knees. I straighten up, trying to regain composure. "What about you? What happened?"

She gently takes my arm and leads me to the couch. I sink down, relief flooding through me as I realize she's safe. As she heads for the kitchen, I try to steady my breathing, my pulse gradually slowing.

She returns with a bottle of water for me. "I may have rejected his advances."

"Men." I roll my eyes. The adrenaline rush fades, leaving me drained.

"The dude smelled like a jar of liquefied BO," she says, twisting her face. "And he hogged the booth for almost two hours! I had to hold my breath every time I walked by."

"Yikes. Where's your roommate?"

"On vacation. Lucky girl has parents who take her to Australia. I'm gonna change out of my uniform real quick. I feel gross."

"I'll text Amber and Chloe. We can have a good old-fashioned sleepover. No way in hell am I leaving you alone tonight."

"Thanks, Sienna."

Half an hour later, V and I lounge on the couches in her

living room, with Amber and Chloe on a makeshift pallet between us.

"We need to do this more often," Amber says. "It's so nice to get a break from the kids."

Amber and I still haven't talked about our fight on Saturday, but I refuse to bring it up and make V's night even worse. I'm good at pretending nothing's wrong. Besides, being here for V is more important.

Chloe stuffs her face with a handful of popcorn, scrolling through Netflix. "I'm jealous of your roommate," she tells V. "I'd love to just drop everything and travel."

"That'll be me one day," V says wistfully. "I can't wait to finally stop showing off my ass and titties for crummy tips."

"Don't you actually have to *have* an ass and titties to do that?" Chloe teases.

V throws a pillow at her head. "That's why I have padding."

"It won't be too much longer," I reassure her. "You'll be done with nursing school in no time."

"I'm counting down the days." She snuggles into the blanket. "No offense, guys, but I'm out of here the second I land a travel nursing role."

"We'll miss ya." I reach across to grab her hand.

She smiles in return.

"At least you're working towards something better," Amber mutters.

Here we go.

"I'm a fucking secretary. The most meaningless job I can think of."

I head to the kitchen to raid V's liquor cabinet as Amber complains about how pointless and boring her job is.

I return empty-handed, and Amber's foul mood casts a shadow over the evening until Chloe finally turns on a show for background noise.

"Well, what do you want to do?" V asks Amber.

"It doesn't matter," she replies miserably. "I need this job for the paycheck. I don't have time to go to a bunch of interviews or go back to college."

I'm getting really sick of her complaining about her life and not doing anything about it. "Just keep your options open. Another job will come along," I say, trying to offer support.

"I can't just wait for the perfect job to fall into my lap. That doesn't happen for everyone. We can't all have the perfect body, perfect job, perfect guy—"

"Wait, perfect guy?" Chloe interjects. "Are you seeing someone?"

I've never been more grateful for a subject change. "Yeah," I say dreamily, thoughts of Liam bringing a smile to my face. "The guy I brought to the bar two weeks ago. He's so great."

"He must be for *you* to be dating him," Chloe says. "Have you fucked him yet, or are you leaving him hanging?"

I look away sheepishly, and the memory of our blasphemous Sunday heats my cheeks.

"Oh my God! You broke your three-year dry spell? When?"

"A couple days ago."

She shakes her head at me. "I never thought I'd see the day."

I roll my eyes. "We haven't defined our relationship or anything yet. We're trying to take things slow."

"Wait, you mean he's not your boyfriend?" Chloe crosses her arms.

"I know what you're thinking—"

"That the pot has been calling the kettle black for months?" Chloe's harsh reaction cuts deep, but I suppose I deserve it.

"I know I'm breaking my rules, but—"

"Let me guess. He's *different*. He *cares about you*. He's not *ready* for a relationship." Her words are meant to sting, and they do.

I open my mouth to respond, but V steps in, coming to my defense.

"Cut her some slack. This guy sounds pretty great, and as long as you like him and he's treating you right, that's all that matters."

"Whatever. This kettle is going to say hi to some pot outside." Chloe heads out the back door to the balcony.

I wrap my arms around my knees. "Can you believe her?" I ask, seeking validation from my friends.

"I mean, it is pretty hypocritical," Amber says.

I stare at her in disbelief. "I thought you'd all be happy for me."

"I am," V assures me.

"Thanks, V." I'm grateful for her support, but I'm still upset by Amber and Chloe's reaction.

I'm not going to waste my breath defending Liam. I can't convince Amber and Chloe that he's different, and I don't need to. He is leagues above the men they choose to give themselves to.

"Okay, okay," Chloe says, walking back in from the balcony. "Let's just drop it and enjoy our night together."

"Agreed." Amber nods. "No more talk about guys."

V claps her hands. "Let's play a game!"

We settle on Uno, but as we laugh and have fun, it feels

surface-level.

Amber is too jealous to talk to me anymore and still hasn't apologized for how she treated me Saturday. Chloe thinks I'm a hypocrite. And if all goes well, V will be traveling the country three months from now. My friend group is falling apart at the seams, and I don't know how to keep it together.

Chapter 27
Sienna

I walk the track on the upper level after my beginner's class, taking out my phone to drop Riley a message. Nathan's girlfriend was due to join my class this morning, but she never showed.

> **ME**
> Hey, Riley. Missed you in class today. Hope everything is okay.

> **RILEY**
> Yeah, sorry. My boss let me sit in on a meeting, so I couldn't leave.

> **ME**
> No worries. If you're free now, I could give you a private lesson.

> **RILEY**
> I have 12:15 to 12:25 free, but that's my lunch break.

> **ME**
> How about I bring lunch to you at your office? We can just catch up.

RILEY

I'm flattered you think I have an office. That'd be great, though, thanks.

She sends me the name and address of the firm where she's interning, and we agree to meet there in half an hour. As I finish my laps, my mind shifts to preparing for our meet-up.

Riley seems driven and focused, the type to tackle challenges head-on. I'll have to take a page out of her book if I want to convince her I'm not only after Liam's money.

The prospect of gaining a new friend is exciting, though, and I appreciate her making time for me in her busy schedule.

A short while later, I enter the sleek, professional building, carrying a paper bag of takeout. Riley finds me in the lobby, looking polished in a burgundy button-up blouse tucked into a pencil skirt paired with classy black pumps.

"Wow, you look great," I compliment sincerely. I look down at my own outfit, suddenly feeling underdressed in my workout jacket, leggings, and sports bra.

"Thanks," she says with a grateful smile, leading the way to a quiet corner of the break room.

We settle into our chairs, and I pull out two steaming-hot Philly cheesesteaks from the bag.

"These smell incredible. Thank you so much!" Riley exclaims, her eyes lighting up as she unwraps her sandwich.

The break room remains a hub of activity around us, with colleagues bustling in and out, engaged in hushed conversations about cases and clients.

"Food is my love language," she says mid-bite.

"Seems we have something in common."

We're off to a good start, but the professional atmosphere of corporate law highlights the gap between our two worlds.

"I thought we should get to know each other better."

"I think that's a good idea," Riley agrees. "Our first meeting was a little awkward," she says.

"That's an understatement," I joke before getting serious. "Look, I like Liam a lot."

"I can tell. And I know for a fact he likes you, too. I can't deny that there's a connection. I saw it when we were at lunch. But I'm gonna be honest—"

Riley's phone buzzes on the table. She picks it up begrudgingly.

"Sorry, I need to take this."

I continue eating as she talks to a client on the phone. Her demeanor shifts seamlessly into professional mode as she discusses legal matters.

"Yes, ma'am. Yes, ma'am. That's correct, ma'am."

Riley's food sits there getting cold as she continues to reassure the woman on the phone that everything is in hand with her upcoming case. I watch her with admiration; it's clear she's committed to her career.

Once the call ends, she turns back to me. "Sorry about that," she tells me, putting her phone away.

"No worries. What were you gonna say?"

"Oh right," she continues. "Liam—"

"Knock knock!" a colleague of hers calls out as he enters the room. "Did you finish the brief from last week?"

She nods. "It's on my desk."

He lingers by our table, asking more questions about the case, even though it sounds like it has been completed. My frustration mounts at his rudeness.

"Excuse me," I say politely. "Riley is on break, and she only has a few minutes to eat. Do you mind?"

"Sorry, I'll let you finish," he says before making a hasty retreat.

Once he's gone, Riley turns to me. "Thanks. You'd think as a future lawyer I'd be more assertive."

"Don't worry about it."

I want to press her about what she was going to say about Liam, but I'm conscious that her break will finish soon, and I want her to have time to eat.

Fortunately, she brings it up unprompted. "As I was saying, when Liam gives his heart away, he *really* gives it away. There's no in-between for him. It's all or nothing. I just don't want him to go through another heartbreak so soon after the last one."

Her words give me pause. If there's no in-between for him, why does it feel like that's exactly where we are? Somewhere between friends and more than friends.

"How will I know? If he feels that way about me, I mean?"

"Oh, you'll know," she assures me. "Trust me."

As we eat, she tells me more about what her job involves, from drafting legal documents to sitting in on high-stakes meetings. It's clear she's very bright and passionate about her work.

"It's a lot of work for a little pay, but I'm really grateful for this internship. I have to make it a priority, even if that means skipping Pilates classes."

"I understand. It sounds like you're gaining valuable experience here."

A man in a suit stops in the doorway. "Ms. Porter, meet me at my desk to deliver a progress update."

"Yes, sir."

Riley stands as she shoves the last bite of food into her mouth. She wipes her mouth with a napkin before collecting her things.

"Liam can be... intense. He needs someone who will match his commitment. So, if that's not you, you should back out now before he gets too attached." She walks toward the door, stopping to turn around in the doorway. "I have to get back to work. Thanks again for lunch. It was nice getting to know you better."

"Same here," I reply, standing up. "Let's do this again sometime."

"Definitely," she says with a smile.

I leave the firm feeling optimistic about my budding friendship with Riley. Our meet-up went well, but I'm not sure if she's entirely convinced I'm the right person for Liam. There will be plenty of time for her to come around. I don't plan on going anywhere.

Chapter 28
Liam

One day without Sienna, and my mind was made up.

Last night, sitting on my living room couch, I read her text over and over. One of her friends needed help, so I couldn't come over. It was a simple message, nothing out of the ordinary, but the pang of disappointment hit me hard.

That evening spent at home alone made me realize I didn't want to go a single day without seeing her. I kept glancing at my phone, hoping for another message from her, something to hold me over until I could see her again.

Now, as I browse the jewelry store, I feel myself going down that familiar path again. The path where I fall head over heels and start dreaming of forever.

The jewelry in the display cases shimmers under the bright lights as I move through the store.

I'm not looking for an engagement ring, although I did peruse the ring case—just for a minute.

One step at a time. I need to ask her to be my girlfriend first.

"Can I help you?" a woman in professional attire asks me.

"I'm looking for a gold necklace, ideally with a teardrop-shaped diamond," I reply, trying to convey the image I have in my mind.

She nods and guides me to a display case toward the back. Opening the glass door, she pulls out a necklace that matches my description, but it's still not quite what Sienna was wearing.

"Do you have one with a thinner chain? One that goes through the diamond? I'm trying to match a necklace I know my girlfriend likes."

"Ah, that would be a floating diamond. We don't have one in that particular style in stock, but you can make a custom order."

"No, I need this today." I peruse the nearby cases, spotting a necklace that looks similar to what I'm envisioning but with a circular diamond. "What about this one? I think she'll like that." The necklace catches the light just right, and in my mind's eye, I can see it resting perfectly against Sienna's collarbone.

"Excellent choice, sir. Solid gold—"

"Yeah, I'll take it," I say, impatient to see Sienna again.

The woman carries the necklace to the register and rings it up. I don't hesitate to swipe my card for the five-hundred-dollar purchase, and I walk out of the store and hop into my truck.

Next stop, the coffee shop where we met.

The familiar aroma of coffee brings back memories of our first date, and I walk out with a double chocolate mocha in a drink carrier, the same drink she ordered that day. I decide to pick up a bouquet of flowers from a street vendor en route to her apartment, selecting a bouquet with a variety of white flowers. I'll have to find out what her favorite flower is for next time.

I stand outside Sienna's apartment with the flowers and coffee, keeping the jewelry box in my pocket. She opens the door with a smile, her eyes lighting up when she sees me.

"This is for you," I tell her as she steps aside to let me in, holding out the drink carrier with the flowers resting on it.

She holds her hands over her heart. "You got these for me?" she gushes. She carries it to the kitchen as I take my boots off.

After putting the flowers in a vase of water and displaying them in the center of the table, she crosses the room to me.

"You are so sweet. I love them." She wraps her arms around my waist. "What's the occasion?"

"I missed you yesterday."

"I missed you too. Who knew you were such a sap?" she teases, gazing up at me.

"I'm not a sap. I just want to treat my girl right."

"Your girl?" she removes her arms from around me.

I freeze at her reaction. I can't read her face, and suddenly I'm doubting everything. "My... girlfriend," I say awkwardly. "I thought... if you wanted—"

She loops her fingers through my belt loops and pulls me in by my pelvis, crushing her lips against mine.

Her brazen manhandling erases any doubts and ignites a fire inside me. I grip her hips and lift her, carrying her to the bedroom with her legs wrapped around me.

We enter her room, and a soft breeze lifts the white curtains. She throws her head back and laughs, the sound like music to my ears as I spin her around the light and airy room. Elation washes over me, and nothing could ruin this moment.

Her thigh shifts against the pocket of my jeans, and she lifts her head back up and locks gazes with me. "Okay, what is poking me in the leg?"

"Oh, yeah," I say, setting her down. She lands delicately on her feet, reminding me that she used to be a cheerleader. I wonder if she still has her uniform...

Focus.

I take a deep breath and pull out the jewelry box, watching her expectantly.

She takes it hesitantly and opens it, the color draining from her face.

Not the reaction I expected.

"It's solid gold with a real diamond."

She remains silent.

"I tried to match the one you had on a couple days ago."

She hasn't moved. Hasn't taken her eyes off the necklace.

I slowly take it back from her. "You don't like it."

She looks up at me, eyes wide. "It's beautiful! Thank you. It's just..." She shakes her head. "We just had sex a few days ago."

I look back and forth from her to the necklace in my hand, wondering what the hell those things have to do with each other.

"Are you saying it's too soon for a gift like this?"

"Yes, that. We've barely known each other a month. Don't you think that's a little fast?"

No. This is me taking it slow. I wanted to buy her a car.

"It's not just that." She lowers her head, and I can't stand seeing her look so lost, so fragile—I want my vibrant, confident Sienna back. "I've never told anyone this..."

Sensing she's about to tell me something serious, I guide her to the bed, and we sit on the edge, facing each other.

She wraps her arms around herself, steeling herself to speak. I stay silent, determined to give her all the time she needs to get this out.

"I was dating this guy, Austin."

My fists clench at the sound of her ex-boyfriend's name crossing her perfect lips.

"He tended to be very... transactional about sex," she says quietly. "It was subtle at first—he'd take me out to a nice restaurant, then initiate sex when we got home—but towards the end of our relationship, he got bolder. If he took me out to dinner or bought me anything, he would expect to be... repaid."

My fists clench at my sides, anger rising in my chest, but I try to keep my cool. The last thing she needs is me losing it when she's opening up about something so painful.

"And then one day..." Her breath catches in her throat as her eyes begin to water. "He took me out for lunch and to my favorite store for their half-off candle sale."

Her shoulders slump, and I instinctively rub her back.

"I picked out five candles. We thought they were ten dollars each, but when they rang them up, they came up twenty each. They said the sale hadn't started yet." She shakes her head, lost in the memory. "I offered to put some back, but he said it was fine, and he paid for all of them. We got home and sat on the couch. I told him how much I appreciated the candles, and he said..." Her eyes well up with tears, and her bottom lip quivers. "'Why don't you show me how much you appreciate it.' And he unbuttoned his pants."

My heart sinks as tears fall down her face.

"I just did it," she says, shaking her head. "I didn't want to, but he guilted me into it." Tears fall freely down her cheeks. "And when I was done, he lifted the bag and said..." She takes a deep breath. "'Here, you earned it.'"

I throw the necklace to the side and wrap my arms around her. She buries her head in my chest, sobbing.

"I felt disgusting. Ashamed."

I rest my head on top of hers, stroking her back, trying to soothe her shaking. After a few minutes, she calms down.

"That was the last straw. I was tired of being treated like a prostitute. I told him to get the fuck out." She laughs humorlessly, wiping her eyes with the back of her hand. "I vowed that day to never let anyone demean me like that again. I started demanding respect, respecting myself."

I press a gentle kiss to her forehead, loosening my hold but continuing to stroke her back. She's been through so much, my Sienna, and yet she's so damn strong.

She straightens, finally meeting my eyes. "It was a long time ago. I know you've been paying for dinner and stuff like that, but I knew you weren't like him. I'm not comparing you to him, of course. I guess it was something about receiving an expensive gift right after we started having sex that triggered something for me."

I let the information sink in. I had no idea she went through something like that.

"I just don't want to owe anyone anything."

I cup her face in my hands. "You don't owe me anything. Ever," I tell her, imploring her with my eyes to believe me.

She lowers her head in sadness.

No, not sadness. *Shame*.

I lift her head back up, forcing her to meet my gaze. "You didn't owe *him* anything either, Sienna. What he did was abusive. You did nothing wrong. He was the jerk."

"Yeah, and I was the idiot. I let him degrade me. Convince

me that my worth, my dignity, was worth a bag of candles and a fucking salad."

The absolute defeat on her face breaks my heart, and I would do anything to erase her pain. I glance over at the necklace on the bed, feeling uneasy.

She follows my gaze. "You can take it back," she says sadly, her voice barely above a whisper.

"I'm not taking it back." I pick up the necklace in one hand and wrap my other hand around hers, guiding her to the mirror across the room. Our reflections look back at us, our emotions raw.

I gently move her hair to the side, standing behind her. Our eyes lock in the mirror, and she gives me a soft smile.

"I bought this because I wanted to, Sienna. That's all. I care about you, and I wanted to get you something that I knew you would like. I don't expect anything in return. I just want to make you happy."

I take the necklace out of the box, lowering it in front of her collarbone and clasping it around the back.

She moves her hair out of the way and places a hand on the diamond. "You don't have to buy me diamond necklaces. I just want to spend time with you."

Her vulnerability pulls on my heart.

"I understand that." I lower my head to whisper in her ear. "But no girlfriend of mine is wearing fake jewelry." I keep my tone light, but I mean every word. "You deserve the best. I want to be the one to give it to you."

Sienna looks at her reflection with misty eyes, but a genuine smile spreads across her face. She runs her fingers over the delicate chain, tracing the diamond with her fingertips.

"It's beautiful," she says softly.

"Not as beautiful as you."

"You sap," she teases, and I wrap my arms around her waist.

"I just want you to know that this necklace, or anything I buy you, is not about expecting anything in return. I just want to show you how much I care about you."

She looks down at the necklace, then back up at me. Her eyes soften, and she turns around to kiss me. She rests her head on my chest, and we stand there wrapped in each other's arms.

"I care about you too. You're everything I could ever want in a boyfriend."

I press a tender kiss to her forehead. "I love hearing you call me that."

She tilts her face up and grins at me, wrapping her arms around the back of my neck and kissing me.

"You know, I never even lit those candles. They're still up there in my closet." She nods her head to the paper bag on the top shelf. "They just remind me."

I walk to the closet, grab the bag from the shelf, and set it on the dresser.

She pulls a couple of candles out, a mischievous grin spreading on her face. "Want to help me say 'fuck you' to Austin?" she says, her voice dripping with naughtiness.

I match her smirk and take a lighter out of my pocket. "Way ahead of you."

Chapter 29
Liam

Pumpkin Cinnamon Bun

With the candle lit and the wax beginning to melt, Sienna takes a small step away from me and slowly removes her top to reveal a white lacy bra. She tosses the shirt across the room and smiles at me in challenge. I stalk over to her and cup her face, pressing my pelvis to hers as I kiss her deeply.

She giggles playfully and loops her fingers in my belt loops, pulling me closer. Rising on her toes, she presses her tits against my chest, and I remove my shirt and turn her to face the mirror. Standing behind her, I run my hands up and down her stomach, cupping her tits as she turns her head for a kiss.

I turn her head back to the mirror so she can watch as I kiss her neck and trail my hand down to her athletic shorts. She rests her head against my chest with a dreamy look on her face as I rub over her pussy.

I spin her around quickly, and she raises a leg to straddle me, cupping my jaw as I massage her ass cheek. My needy girl grinds against my jeans, craving the friction. I slap her ass with one hand and bury the other in her soft blonde hair.

She pulls away from the kiss to watch us in the mirror. She smiles at what she sees and bites her lip before slowly touching the waistline of her tight shorts. My fingertips rest on her waist as she drops the shorts, not wanting to stop touching her for even a second.

She bends forward slightly, causing her tits to spill out the top of her bra, and I step behind her, gripping her hips clad in white lacy panties. She grinds her ass against me as if we're dancing in a club, and my dick gets painfully hard in my jeans. With a naughty smile, Sienna lowers her bra just enough to reveal her nipples, rubbing them, massaging them, and pushing her tits together.

I grip her hips tighter and slam my own into her over and over, giving her a taste of what's to come. The slapping sounds of our bodies ramming together elicit a moan from her.

Turning her around to face me again, I sit on the edge of the bed and place kisses on her toned stomach. My hands reach around to her ass, and I move my head to the side to take in the sight of her tight ass in the mirror. I massage it, lifting her cheeks, but there's not much give. To not spend time appreciating her perfect ass would be a crime.

She cups my jaw with both hands and throws her head back as one of my hands travels back around to the front, stroking her pussy over her panties. She moans beautifully as I rub her clit, feeling her wetness under my fingertips.

Standing, I turn her to face the mirror with a hand over the front of her throat. I rest it there gently, but my fingers strum a different tune. I plunge two fingers inside her pussy, fingering her roughly. I move my fingers in and out as hard as I can, and her moans grow louder and louder.

I stare at her parted lips in the mirror, the sounds of my fingers in her pussy echoing through the small room. I lower my hand from her neck to her tit and grope it harshly, then remove my fingers and turn her once more, using one hand to lower her panties just enough for the other hand to rub her clit.

Bending my head to kiss and lick her tit, I take some into my teeth, biting hard enough to leave a mark as she rides my fingers. Her moans grow louder, turning me on as much as the wetness coating my fingers.

I step back with a satisfied smirk, and she reaches for my pants. We kiss softly as she lowers them, and as I step out, she bounces on the balls of her feet eagerly. I catch sight of her ass bouncing in the mirror as I remove my pants from around my feet.

She is absolute perfection. She tosses her hair over her shoulders and moves to lower herself. Before she can, I cup her face, kissing her passionately. As we kiss, she rubs her hand over the outline of my dick. I won't keep her waiting any longer.

I push her down by her shoulders so that she's kneeling in front of me. My hands tangle in her messy hair as I hold it in a makeshift ponytail, and she lowers my underwear to my feet. She takes me into her mouth, but her body is stiff. She shifts her weight from knee to knee.

She must be uncomfortable kneeling on the hardwood floor. I could move us to the rug. No, I've got a better idea. I remove her head from my cock and guide her to the bed. Taking a chance, I step onto the bed, wearing nothing but black crew socks.

I'm waiting for her to ask what the fuck I'm doing standing on the bed, but she gets the idea and kneels in front of me on the mattress. From this height, I can see her entire body in the mirror, her white matching bra and panties making her tan skin stand out.

Sienna bobs her head back and forth expertly, and I watch us in the mirror. Every inch of her skin is flawless, glowing in the evening sun streaming through the window. I hold up her hair in one hand, leaving two messy strands framing her pretty face.

She lifts higher on her knees, and I know she's about to deepthroat my cock. She takes it deeper and deeper until her nose touches my lower stomach, but instead of pulling away, she nuzzles her tits into my balls.

The sight of us in the mirror, the feeling of her throat around my cock, the sensation of her soft tits rubbing against my sensitive balls is too much. I can't hold back the release, and I come deep into her mouth.

I breathe through the release, and she takes it all—every drop. She pulls her head away and looks up at me, opening her mouth to show me the cum on her tongue. She giggles in euphoria as she throws herself down onto the pillows, her arms spread wide.

Vanilla Pumpkin Waffles

When I arrive the next day, Sienna opens the door wearing a white satin lingerie dress. I'm sure there's a name for it, but my mind is blank at the moment. I close the door quickly—no one gets to see her like this but me.

My gaze travels from her pretty face to the diamond necklace, then to her nipples poking through the sheer fabric. I shake my head slowly. "You are so perfect."

She gives me a flirty smile, and I grip the back of her head and press a deep kiss to her lips. Walking her backward to the couch—the bedroom is too far—I lay her down on the soft blanket, her head on the armrest. I kneel on the center of the couch, and she spreads her legs around me. As my fingers travel up her thighs and beneath her nightdress, she puts an index finger in her mouth and gives me a naughty smile—no panties.

I brush my fingers over her bare pussy, and her finger moves from her lips to her nipple over the white fabric. She circles it until it hardens, and I can't help myself. I bend over to suck the nipple, leaving a wet mark on the silky fabric.

Lifting the hem of her dress, I rub two fingers up and down her pussy. She leans back further into the couch, breathing out a moan. My middle finger runs over her clit, then I insert it to the first knuckle. I'm feeling smug as I continue fingering her, enjoying her blissful expression and soft moans.

She licks her lips, drawing my eye to her full, soft lips. She spreads her legs further, one foot on the ground as my finger curls and straightens inside her. Her moans grow louder, and I increase my pace.

"Oh," she breathes.

I remove my finger and rest my hand against her flat stomach, my thumb rubbing over her clit. She wiggles around, escaping my touch. Her sensitive clit pulses with need, but she wriggles out of my grasp.

Smirking, I lower my face between her legs, and she grips my hair and giggles as my beard tickles her inner thighs. I look up at her through my lashes and dart my tongue out to taste her. I keep my tongue flat, and she bounces her body to ride my face as I return the favor of the earth-shattering blow job she gave me yesterday.

Her needy moans grow louder and louder as she massages my head with both hands. She rubs her clit against my tongue, and it doesn't take long for that gush of arousal to coat my beard. She pants as she comes down from the high, and I look at her in amazement.

"Do you have any idea how sexy you are?"

She looks at me like I'm a simple fool and gives a pointed glance at the coffee table where the next candle is burning. I smile and shake my head. She knew we wouldn't make it to the bedroom.

Salted Caramel Swirl

Snuggling in bed the next day, I read Sienna's text over her shoulder. She doesn't try to hide it from me, so I assume it's fine.

It's her friend, Veronica, begging her to come out tonight.

VERONICA
It won't be fun without you!

ME
I'll think about it.

"Do you want to go?" I ask.

"I don't know. Normally I never miss a party, but I want to spend time with you," she says, resting her head on my chest.

VERONICA

Let me guess, you're with your boy toy?

ME

I can't help it. He's fun to play with.

I shake my head, and she puts her phone on the nightstand next to one of her candles.

I kiss her temple. "We could go. If you want."

She raises her eyebrows at me. "You hated it last time we went out with my friends. I thought you weren't a fan of parties."

I shrug. "I've been to a few parties in my day."

She runs a finger up and down my chest. "Hmm... let me guess. You stood off to the side with your grumpy face and watched everyone else play drinking games?"

"My grumpy face?" I ask.

"You know, your usual face." She furrows her brows and sets her lips in a thin line.

I ruffle her hair, rolling my body on top of hers. "You mean this face?" I tease, kissing her all over.

She giggles, pretending to try and fight me off.

"And I'll have you know I actually did play the stupid games," I tell her.

She scrunches her face in mock irritation. "I didn't say I didn't like your grumpy face. I think it's sexy." She runs her nose along my jaw.

"Like your bedhead. Very sexy."

"So we're agreed. We'd have way more fun here than at some party."

"Oh I know we could," I say low in her ear.

She giggles, shoving me off her and grabbing her phone from the nightstand.

VERONICA
Don't leave me here with these two!

ME
You'll have fun without me. I'll try to come out next time.

She returns the phone and straddles me, wrapping her arms around my neck as I sit up to meet her pursed lips.

"You're not worried about me hanging out with your friends after last time, are you?" I ask, suddenly concerned.

"Of course not," Sienna assures me, resting her forehead against my own before letting out a resigned sigh. "To be honest, I was looking for an excuse not to go." She runs her hands through my hair. "Amber and I still haven't made up yet, and I don't want to go out with the group until we've talked it out, you know?"

I rub her back in soothing circles. "You know, if you're worried about Amber, I can always come with you to see her. We could all go out for a walk or something. Give you a chance to talk to her in a casual setting, without the pressure of meeting her one-on-one."

Sienna's breath catches in her throat. "You'd do that for me?"

"Of course."

She might not realize it yet, but I'd do anything for her. And that knowledge? It's terrifying.

"Oh, *Liam*. You did this?" Sienna gushes, her hands over her heart.

I open my arms to showcase what I set up. "Do you like it?"

"Oh my God, I love it!"

She climbs into the bed of the truck parked in an open grassy area next to a creek. She pulls the candle out of her small backpack and sets it down before laying back on the blankets and gazing up at the stars.

I climb in next to her and light the candle before lying on my side to admire her beauty under the moonlight.

"The stars are so beautiful here," she says dreamily. "I could look at them all night."

I love that she loves the farm as much as I do. That'll make her moving in with me much easier next year. I don't want to wait that long. I want this to be my life every day.

She looks over at me. "You're smiling," she states. "You *liiike* me," she singsongs, her honeyed voice matching the color of her hair.

"I really do." I wrap her in my arms, and she nuzzles close to me.

We snuggle closer and stare at the stars, listening to the creek's gentle flow. Her warmth against me, the constellations above—everything feels perfect.

"Did you do anything like this for your ex?" she asks sheepishly, which isn't like her.

"No," I answer simply. "You're the only person I would do this for."

With the candle lit on the bathroom sink, we step into the shower and close the curtain behind us. Hot water cascades over us, and Sienna tilts her head back, letting the water drip down her body. Rivulets stream between her breasts, and I restrain myself from catching them with my tongue.

She runs her hands over her naked body—her neck, her breasts, her stomach. I stand there mesmerized until she cups my neck and presses a soft kiss to my lips. Gripping her waist, I kiss her back before trailing kisses down her cheek and jaw.

She moans and leans her head to the side, and I wrap my hand around one side of her neck and place kisses on the other side, down to her collarbone. She presses her body to mine, and my hard cock pokes her in the stomach as she kisses my neck. I decide right then that neck kissing is my new favorite thing in the world.

We make out under the water, our naked bodies rubbing against each other. My cock lies flat against her, leaking precum on her stomach, but she doesn't seem to mind.

Pulling back, I rest my forehead against hers. "I have a confession."

She looks up at me expectantly.

"This isn't my first time in your shower," I admit in a serious voice. "The first night I stayed here, when I drank too much, I came in here to..."

"Jerk off?" she finishes for me.

I nod slowly.

"I'm not surprised," she says.

"Why not?"

She gives me that signature playful smirk. "Because I'm sexy as hell."

She swipes my precum with her index finger and places it on the center of her tongue.

No argument there.

Chapter 30
Sienna

The hot sun beats down on the pavement as Amber wrangles her two boys out of someone's way.

"Sorry about that," she tells the stranger. "Boys, behave, or you're getting the leash."

The stranger gives her a weird look before continuing on his way.

As we pass a stand selling homemade lotions and creams, I decide to stop and take a look, browsing the products until I hear Amber yelling.

"Hey, put that down. Alright, that's it."

I set down the cream and look over to see Amber strapping backpacks onto the two boys. Leashes extend from the back of the bags, and she attaches the other ends to her wrist with Velcro bracelets.

She returns to me, shaking her head. "Don't judge me," she jokes, but I can sense the underlying exhaustion in her voice.

"I didn't say anything," I say with a smile, hoping to lighten her mood.

We continue down the street with Liam and Anthony chatting behind us. If I know my guy, he's letting Anthony talk and simply taking it all in. Liam doesn't let many people in. I think that's what drew me to him in the first place—the desire to see what he doesn't show anyone else.

Amber and I catch up as we stop at different booths that catch our eye. She apologized profusely to me earlier this morning on the phone and invited Liam and me to join her and Anthony at the farmer's market. This was the perfect idea to give Liam and me a chance to take a break from our routine and Amber and me a chance to reconnect.

I spy a clay ring dish with hand-painted green flowers and stop to pick it up. "This is pretty," I tell the vendor.

She smiles and mutters a thank you.

"So, we're cool, right?" Amber asks at my side.

She keeps the boys tight to her and away from the fragile merchandise. "Of course," I assure her.

Setting the dish on the table, I reach for my wallet to pay.

Liam appears out of nowhere and hands the woman cash. In the past few weeks, he's paid for everything—dinners, groceries, books, even some clothes.

I thank Liam, pressing a kiss to his cheek as the vendor wraps the dish in newspaper. She hands me my purchase, and I gently place it in my shopping bag. Amber's eyes betray a flicker of jealousy before she masks it. I know she's struggling, and part of me wishes I could do more to help. But the other part says those are her issues to deal with, and they have nothing to do with me. Besides, all I do is make her insecurities worse.

As we exit the stand, I turn to her. "I'm sorry too," I tell her. "I didn't mean to brag about my new boyfriend. And I'm sure Anthony can take care of himself."

Amber shakes her head. "I think the reason I got so mad is because everything you said was true," she says, low enough that the boys can't hear, too busy testing the limits of their leashes. She sighs. "Your life is so perfect. You always look stunning, and you have a boyfriend who would buy you anything here."

My life is pretty awesome. But that's because I make my own life awesome. I work hard to look like this, and I went out and found the perfect boyfriend.

I don't know what to say, so we walk in silence. I glance back at Liam and Anthony as Anthony drones on about some superhero movie. Liam looks like he'd rather be anywhere but here.

Amber shakes her head. "I'm sorry. I need to get it together."

She sounds so miserable, I can't stop myself from offering to help. I just hope it won't set her off on another rant.

"Listen, how about I watch the boys while you go shopping with V? You said you wanted to put more effort into your appearance, but you don't have time. V's the best at that stuff. She can do a color analysis on you and get you a cart full of flattering clothes in no time."

She subtly glances down at her attire—one of Anthony's shirts and a pair of worn leggings. "It would be nice to have my own clothes that fit, but Elliot is extremely attached to me right now, and Levi needs glasses, which do not come cheap. I'll probably have to buy multiple pairs over the next few years, too. Maybe when they're a little older, I'll take you up on that."

"I won't be around here for much longer. Liam's moving into his family's farmhouse in February, and I'll probably go with him. I mean, we're already back and forth between each other's houses—"

"Wait, what? Are you serious?" She stops walking and turns to me, causing the boys to bounce back into her.

"What?" I say casually.

"Sienna, you've been dating for less than a month, and

179

you're talking about uprooting your life to live on a *farm*? In the middle of God-knows-where?"

"I know it's fast, but when you know, you know." We continue walking. "I want to be with him, and I love the farm. It's got a cute little farmhouse, and we're taking his dog Zoe with us." Liam and I haven't talked about me moving in with him—or about the future at all, really. But I'm confident enough in our relationship that it'll happen, if not immediately, then soon after he moves.

Amber shakes her head in disbelief. "I can't believe you're gonna be someone's housewife. I don't even know who you are anymore. I thought you wanted to explore different careers and travel."

"Okay, that's a little dramatic. I never said anything about being a housewife. I can still do all that stuff—"

Amber scoffs. "Yeah, sure you can," she says sarcastically. "Take it from me. Babies come before you know it. And then you're stuck."

"You're blowing this way out of proportion."

"What about your career?"

"Pilates is more of a hobby than a career," I explain. "I wouldn't even have to work if I didn't want to, Liam makes plenty of money."

"Oh, so *that's* why you're moving in with him."

"Excuse me?" Now it's my turn to stop us in the middle of the road. "I told you, I care about him. I *want* to be with him. Why can't you just be happy for me?"

Her eyes dart around the people staring at us. "I am. I'm just worried about you."

"Well you have a funny way of showing it." I cross my arms.

Levi tugs at her shirt. "Mommy, there's snow cones." He points across the road.

"One minute, sweetie," she tells him before looking back at me. "Look, I'm sorry. I just feel like this is all too fast. You barely know this guy, and you're talking about moving in with him, miles away from your friends, possibly relying on him for financial stability. It's not safe."

I sigh. "I get it. I'd be worried about you if the roles were reversed."

"I just don't want you to regret anything, and I don't want you to change for some guy."

We walk towards the snow cone vendor.

"He's not just some guy. I really think he's the one."

We join the line, and Amber turns to me. "Then I'm happy for you." She glances back at Anthony and Liam walking toward us. "But seriously, does he ever smile?"

"Not often," I admit with a laugh. "But when he does, it's worth the wait."

Chapter 31
Sienna

With two bags of takeout in hand, I approach an employee at Liam's work.

"Where can I find Liam Wright?"

He points down the hall. "First door on the left."

"Thanks."

Liam texts me during his lunch break every day—noon to one—so I knew exactly when to show up. I had to take an Uber here, but it'll be worth it. I feel a twinge of excitement at seeing his office for the first time. My man is important enough to have his own office, and for some reason, I want to shout it from the rooftops.

His office door is slightly ajar, so I push it open. A woman leans over Liam's desk, bending over so her cleavage nearly touches his face. Liam glares at his computer screen, tapping his fingers on the desk, impatient and annoyed.

The woman doesn't get the hint.

"Okay, I see," she says after he finishes explaining something. "Well, what do you say we get lunch together? I'll buy you a beer for your help," she flirts, even though I know she sees me in the doorway with bags of food.

"Hi there," I say casually, striding confidently into the room.

"Oh! I didn't even notice you," she lies, straightening up

and smoothing her blouse. "I'm Lainey."

Her voice drips with fake sweetness, but her eyes scan me, assessing the competition no doubt.

"Sienna," I introduce myself as I walk toward Liam's desk. "I thought I'd stop by and have lunch with Liam. But if you two are busy..."

"No," Liam says. "She was just leaving."

Lainey bristles at his response but masks it quickly. "Don't mind me. I spend a lot of time in here," she tells me. "I spend so much time in here, everyone at the office calls me his work wife," she jokes with a forced laugh.

I don't pay her any mind as I unpack the food and set the containers on the desk. I try not to show that I'm secretly enjoying her little show.

"How do you know Liam?" she asks, still in the room for some reason.

Her persistence is admirable.

"I'm his girlfriend," I say, not looking at her.

"*Liam!* You never told me you have a *girlfriend*," she says with feigned enthusiasm. "He *never* talks about you, I had no idea. Like, seriously, he *never* talks about you." I refrain from rolling my eyes at her obvious and pathetic attempt to stir something. Instead, I hand Liam his burger and perch on the edge of his desk, facing him. He ignores her and opens his container lid.

"Thanks, angel," he says, giving me a soft smile, which I'm sure is more than he's ever given her.

The way he looks at me—with genuine affection— probably makes her blood boil.

She awkwardly walks around his desk toward the door. "I

guess I'll get out of here then."

She waits for a response, but Liam and I are already stuffing our faces with greasy food.

"You're still my date for the team-building barbecue, right?"

Liam dips a fry in ketchup and lifts it to my mouth, completely ignoring her.

"Okay, I'll see you later."

She finally leaves. She probably gives me a dirty look, but my back is turned.

I chew a fry and pump my eyebrows at him. "Work wife, huh?"

He rolls his eyes and licks salt off his fingers. "Those two words irritate me beyond belief."

He watches me for a reaction, but I just eat my food. I'm not sure what he expects me to say.

"You don't seem to care."

I raise an eyebrow at him. "Care about what?"

"That a woman was in my office, shoving her tits in my face. Aren't you jealous?"

"Ha!"

He looks at me deadpan.

"Wait, you were serious?"

"Of course I'm serious. You're my girlfriend."

"So?" I say casually, taking a sip from our soda.

He gives me a look of disbelief, then shakes his head. I know him well enough now to spot the frustration in his eyes.

I set the soda down. "What do you want me to say?"

"I don't know, but I expected you to be at least a little annoyed. It's like you couldn't care less."

He picks up his burger and takes a bite, avoiding my gaze. His words betray his hurt, something I haven't seen from him before.

"You want me to act all controlling and possessive? Liam, that's not who I am."

He simply continues eating. I can tell my indifference to that woman's flirting upsets him.

"Why would I care if some woman has a crush on you? She's probably not the only one. You're smart, attractive, hardworking. She'd be stupid not to at least try."

He seems to soften a little. "I just think jealousy is the natural reaction when someone else shows interest in your boyfriend. You should care that someone wants to take me away from you."

"Jealousy isn't a sign of love or commitment. It's insecurity masked as something different. I'm not insecure, so I'm not jealous," I explain, hoping he understands so we can drop this.

He sets his burger down and looks at me. "Still, it'd be nice to know you're not indifferent to me."

"You want me to start drama with some woman you work with so you can feel secure? I thought you were more mature than that."

He bristles at my words, and I immediately regret them.

I sigh and set my food down. "I'm sorry. I'm just not the jealous type. And frankly, I don't understand women who are. I'm confident in our relationship, but if some other woman 'tempts' you away, then she can have you. I want someone who is one hundred percent committed to me."

"I am, Sienna. I'm not going anywhere."

"I am, too. So, let's do this," I tell him, taking his hand. "Me and you."

"Me and you," he repeats. He sits up in his chair to kiss me but lowers himself back down.

My shoulders drop. "Why didn't you kiss me?"

"Because I know better than to get between you and chicken nuggets," he jokes.

I roll my eyes. "I bit your hand *one* time."

The tension melts away, and a slight smile creeps onto his face.

"Aw, babe," I tease, "our first fight."

He finishes up the last of his burger. "Does that mean it's time to make up?"

"Did you say make up or make out?" I tease, moving my food to the side.

"Isn't that the same thing in this case?"

Chapter 32
Sienna

Liam and I climb into the truck at the same time, our doors closing in unison. The synchronized motion makes me smile as I realize just how in tune we've become.

"Ready?" he asks, his brown eyes gleaming with excitement.

I nod, and we dump out our grocery bags of snacks between us. A colorful array of salty, sweet, sour, and chocolaty snacks spills out. We picked out each other's favorites to surprise each other, and I'd say we did a pretty good job. My heart flutters at the sight of some of my favorites.

"We better eat the chocolate ones first so they don't melt," I suggest as he pulls out of the parking space.

The truck's engine rumbles, and we garner some attention from others as we drive away from the store.

"Can't argue with that," he agrees, holding out his hand for some chocolate-covered peanuts.

I place a few in his palm, my fingers brushing his skin.

We ride on the highway, our suitcases in the back seat. Liam is taking me to his family's lake house for Fourth of July weekend. Liam arranged for a friend to house-sit and keep an eye on Zoe. I'll miss having her with us, but she would hate the fireworks, so she's safer staying home. It'll be my first time meeting his parents, but I'm not worried.

"Listen." Liam clears his throat, his tone serious. "There's something I need to get off my chest."

I turn the radio down. "What is it?"

"When you first messaged me, I was in a bad place," he starts, his eyes fixed on the road.

"Because of your ex?"

"Yeah." His grip tightens on the steering wheel. "I was depressed. I felt pathetic. Lonely."

I keep quiet, bracing myself for whatever he's about to confess. My mind races with possibilities.

"I agreed to meet you because I wanted a fling. I wanted someone sexy and fun to fool around with. To show off to my friends. I thought that was all this would be."

I nod slowly, processing his words before I reply. "So... you thought I was attractive and agreed to meet with me. What's wrong with that?"

"I don't think you understand." He takes a deep breath before continuing, his voice heavy with regret. "I didn't want a relationship with you. I just wanted to have sex with you," he says, as if it pains him to tell me this. "It had been so long, I'd forgotten what it felt like. I was planning to use you to pull myself out of a funk." He shakes his head, disgusted with himself. "I thought, once I felt confident again, I would find someone else who was actually girlfriend material."

His words sting, but I forge ahead. "When did you change your mind about me?" I ask quietly.

"Pretty quickly, actually. I realized you weren't shallow like I thought you'd be."

"Oh," I say simply, my heart aching.

"I thought you were a girly girl. A city girl who'd never get her hands dirty. I thought you'd be shallow and reckless. But I was so, so wrong. About everything."

His brutal honesty stirs a whirlwind of emotions inside me: hurt at his initial judgment, satisfaction that I got him to change his mind, and guilt that I did something worse.

"That's why I wanted to slow down. I was suddenly terrified that I'd mess up a relationship I never intended to care about. After that first coffee date, I was already falling, but when we fell in the pond, I knew I was done for. I hope you don't look at me differently," he says, genuinely pained by his admission.

I shake my head, my heart aching at the pain in his expression. "Never," I assure him. "You could never make me think badly of you, Liam. You didn't do anything wrong."

But I had.

I had done something far worse.

It's on the tip of my tongue to tell him the truth—that I found him on LinkedIn, not Instagram. That I was looking for an attractive man with a high salary, and he fit the bill.

He reaches for my hand and lifts it to his lips, kissing the top of it. "I just don't want there to be any secrets between us."

This is my chance to confess. Now would be the perfect time to tell him. The weight of my secret presses down on my chest, making it hard to breathe.

But I can't bring myself to do it.

I don't want to cause him more heartache or break his trust in me. He thought I was shallow at first. I don't want to prove him right.

Besides, it's all in the past.

I'm not with him for his money, and that's a fact.

"None whatsoever," I say, guilt sitting like lead in my stomach.

We continue driving and listening to music—a playlist Liam made of the songs I mentioned I like. I start to gather up the snack wrappers, looking for somewhere to stash them.

"Oh, this thing lifts?" I tuck the cupholders into the dash until it clicks closed, clearing the foot area under the middle seat. "That's a nice feature. Makes road head a lot easier," I joke.

"Road head?" he says as if the words are foreign to him.

"Yeah, road head. You know, a blow job in the car?"

He shakes his head. "I didn't know that was a thing."

I look at him in shock. "Don't tell me you've never got road head before?"

He shakes his head again. His innocence is endearing, if not a little surprising.

"Well, we'll have to fix that right now."

His brows furrow in confusion. "Right now? But I'm driving."

I can't help but giggle at his innocence as I unbuckle my seatbelt, the thrill of introducing him to something new making my heart race.

"Wait, you're gonna give me a blow job *while* I'm driving?"

"Uh-huh." I lower myself to my knees in front of the middle seat.

He adjusts in his seat, allowing me to pull his pants down. "Fuck, angel, you're too sexy to be real."

Chapter 33
Liam

I park the truck in my usual spot outside the lake house, taking Sienna's hand and rubbing it gently with my thumb. "Are you nervous?"

"About what?" she asks, tilting her head.

"Meeting my parents," I say as if it should be obvious.

She shrugs. "Not really."

I shake my head. "Your confidence is astounding."

She gives me an innocent smile.

As we step out of the truck, I go to grab the bags from the back seat. "Just so you know, my parents are very traditional. Old-fashioned," I inform her as she comes around the truck to me.

Sienna squeezes my free hand. "You have nothing to worry about. Parents love me."

She rises on her toes to kiss me, her lips soft and pliant as always, prompting me to deepen the kiss. Even though she isn't worried, I am. My parents adored Anna, and Sienna is her polar opposite. I decided not to mention that to her. I want her to be herself, and I didn't want to make her insecure. But now that I think about it, I don't think that word is even in her vocabulary.

Sienna waits for me at the front door, and I open it and step inside, lugging our two suitcases. She follows behind me in her

V-neck sundress, the white corset top hugging her chest and showing just a little bit of cleavage, the skirt flowing out in a pink and white flower pattern. She looks like a breath of fresh air, summertime embodied.

I set our stuff down in the entryway and find my mom in the kitchen. Nerves cause my stomach to roll as I prepare to introduce Sienna.

"There's my other boy!" Mom exclaims.

Sienna steps out from behind me, and my mom's eyebrows shoot up in surprise.

"You must be Sienna! I thought you weren't coming."

Mom has the same light brown hair as Nathan, streaked with a few grays. She wears it straight, and it hangs just past her shoulders.

"I told you she was coming," I say, feeling a little defensive.

Mom wraps me in a quick hug before stepping back. "Well, I'm glad you came, Sienna. I'm Jill."

She smiles as she takes in Sienna, from her beautiful blonde hair to the sandals on her feet.

"Why didn't you think she was coming?" I ask.

"Nathan said he passed you on the highway, but you were by yourself."

I freeze. Heat creeps up my neck. "Oh, I... We..."

I turn to Sienna for help, but she simply stands there, a subtle smirk on her face. My eyes plead with her to help me come up with an explanation.

Heat rises to my cheeks as my mom looks back and forth between the two of us, and Sienna crosses her arms, that self-satisfied smirk gracing her lips. She's letting me flounder—payback for not saving her when Nathan and Riley caught us on the back porch.

"I was laying down," Sienna finally says, saving me. "I get real carsick."

Relief floods through me, and I pray Mom didn't notice my reaction and come to her own conclusion.

Mom nods. "Ah, I see. Well, we'll get you some Dramamine before we go out on the boat tomorrow." She pats Sienna on the shoulder.

"I'm gonna take our stuff up to the rooms." I quickly grab our suitcases and head for the stairs, more than happy to get out of the kitchen.

I feel bad for leaving Sienna alone with my mom, but I have no doubt she can handle herself. How is it that I'm more nervous about this weekend than she is?

I drop Sienna's bag outside the room she'll share with Riley and head into my own room, finding my brother at the open window. He's flicking the ash off a joint, and the scent immediately hits my nose.

I close the door and set my bag on the bed. "You're crazy," I tell him, shaking my head. "Dad's probably outside somewhere. You know he'll smell that."

"Dude, I'm on the top floor. Smoke goes up," he says, as if I'm the idiot here.

"Glad college is teaching you something."

He holds the joint out for me, but I shake my head. I tried it in college—didn't care for it.

"So..." Nathan drags out the word suggestively.

I cross my arms and look at him. "What?"

He pumps his brows. "You and your girlfriend," he teases.

"What about us?"

"Dude, just spit it out. Are you fucking or what?"

I should be used to his brashness by now, but for some reason it still surprises me.

I don't answer.

"From what I saw on your porch, I imagine the answer is yes?"

I remain silent.

"I'll take that as a yes." He grins proudly. "It's about time! How long has it been?"

I roll my eyes. "Three years."

"God damn! Not since *college*?"

Why do I even bother talking to him? "Nope, and not that it's any of your business, but it's been three years for her too."

"Really? Sounds like a match made in heaven."

He has no idea how right he is.

I stand in the middle of the room, and he just stares at me, expecting more details.

"Can we not talk about my sex life?" I say, exasperated.

"What else matters? You finally have one after *three* years."

"I'm out of here." I leave him in our room, closing the door behind me.

Downstairs, I find my dad and Sienna at the kitchen table. She seems comfortable sitting there with him, the man I got my dark hair and eyes from, though his face is more round. I join my mom in the kitchen to help prep burgers, picking up bits and pieces of Dad and Sienna's conversation as I slice tomatoes.

"Oh, he's been a perfect gentleman."

"Glad to hear that. I like to think I raised my boys right."

She says something in a flirty tone, getting a laugh from my dad. Should I think that's weird?

I set the plate of tomatoes aside and dump a bag of shredded lettuce into a bowl.

"What are you drinking?" she asks him.

"It's a cinnamon whiskey," he answers, setting down his glass. "It's not very good. I'm just trying to get through the bottle."

"I might be able to work with that."

Sienna comes to the kitchen and roots through the fridge, pulling out a can of vanilla cream soda. I gently grab her arm to stop her. "Are you okay with my dad drinking whiskey?" I say quietly so Mom doesn't hear.

Sienna touches my arm. "Yeah, it's okay," she assures me.

She returns to the table and hands the soda to Dad. "Try mixing it with this."

He pops the top, pours the soda into his glass of whiskey and ice, and swirls it. I've never seen him mix whiskey with anything. He labels himself a connoisseur—not in a pretentious way, he just knows what he's talking about.

He swirls the glass again before taking a sip. "Oh, that's much better. Liam, get in here. We can drink our after-dinner whiskey now."

I lock eyes with Sienna, silently checking in. She gives me a subtle nod and a smile.

I grab two glasses and fill them with ice, one for me and one for Sienna. I sit next to Dad across from Sienna, and he pours the cinnamon whiskey and soda.

Sienna and I raise our glasses at the same time, taking a sip together. We both smile at the taste.

"Impressive," I tell her. "You worked a miracle—that

whiskey was gross."

"It was a gift," Dad explains. He's also not quick to smile. I guess that's where I get it from.

Sienna chuckles. "Well, we'll have to find you some better whiskey next time."

He raises his glass. "To finding the good stuff," he toasts.

"To finding the good stuff," we echo, clinking our glasses.

As we sip our drinks, warmth spreads through me that has nothing to do with the alcohol. This is what I've been missing—my family, this sense of belonging. I hope Sienna feels that, too.

"So, Sienna," Mom pipes up from the kitchen, "what do you do for a living?"

"I teach Pilates," she begins before describing her job in detail.

I sit back, watching her effortlessly charm my parents.

In this moment, all my worries fade away.

Chapter 34
Sienna

The smoke from the bonfire rises and curls lazily into the night sky, the orange light casting flickering shadows on the stone fire pit between the house and the water's edge. Our group of six sits around in comfortable chairs, positioned in a circle around the crackling flames.

Riley and I opted for strawberry seltzers while the men across from us drink whiskey. The three of them finished the cinnamon bottle and have moved on to another. I know how some men get when they drink whiskey, but I trust Liam completely. I feel safe here.

Liam reclines comfortably, spreading his legs wide in his chair, owning the space around him. His quiet confidence draws me to him, and if we were alone, I'd make my way to him and sit across his lap.

As the night wears on, the stories come out. I listen to one after the other, each one about Liam and Nathan's childhood. The drunker we all get, the more stories come out.

Jill, Liam's mom, must be pretty tipsy, given her animation as she recounts the story of the time Liam tried to jump into their pool in the backyard.

"He jumped over the side, but his trunks got caught on the ladder, and he fell face-first into the pool and scraped his penis against the ladder!"

I gasp and cover my mouth with my hands.

"He popped his head out of the water, covering himself with his hands, yelling, 'I hurt my penis!'"

Everyone bursts into a fit of laughter, except Liam, who wears his usual grumpy expression. My abs ache from laughing so hard, and even Liam shakes his head with a slight smile.

"I was only seven. That experience scarred me."

Of course, not literally. I haven't noticed any scars.

As we calm down from our laughter, Jill shares a couple more stories from the boys' childhood, giving me a glimpse into the differences between the two brothers.

I can't help but steal glances at Liam, noticing how his stoic demeanor gives way to visible amusement. His rugged charm and quiet intensity have me unable to look away.

Eventually, we retreat into smaller conversations. Nathan and Liam chat while Riley and I discuss the best places to shop for clothes.

As we talk, I'm distracted by Liam. He lifts his whiskey glass to his lips, swirling the amber liquid in his mouth before swallowing. His Adam's apple bobs, and I imagine him walking behind my chair, lifting my head back by my hair, and spitting whiskey into my mouth.

I shake my head and try to focus on what Riley is saying. Something about trying to find professional clothes that are also comfy. I nod to keep her talking, but my eye is drawn to Liam again.

Nathan passes him a cigar, and I can't look away as Liam's cheeks hollow slightly as he sucks in the earthy, sweet taste. He lowers the cigar, holding it between two fingers, and savors the flavor before exhaling a plume of smoke into the night sky.

He looks distinguished as hell in his boots and jeans. At only twenty-four years old, he's more mature than any other man I've met.

I imagine laying him down tonight, kissing every inch of his sexy-as-fuck beard, and—

"—you know what I mean?" Riley finishes.

I snap back to reality and peel my gaze away from Liam, locking eyes with her. Her hazel eyes are slightly glossy and bloodshot.

"Why are you blushing?" she asks. She looks back and forth from Liam to me. "Oh, I see."

She looks over at Jill and Patrick, who are engrossed in their own conversation, paying us no mind.

Once she sees they aren't looking, she pumps her arms back and forth at her sides, a silent way of asking if Liam and I have had sex yet.

I blush harder and nod, feeling a bit awkward talking about this with his parents only five feet from me.

She squeals, practically kicking her feet. "Oh my god!"

"Shh," I caution. "Liam says his parents are very traditional."

"Oh, they are. Patrick *flipped* on us when he caught us smoking weed. And we're twenty years old, for God's sake!" she whispers. "That's also why you and I are in the same room, and Nathan and Liam are in the other. Until we're married, at least."

We chat a while longer, moving on to more appropriate topics until the bonfire dwindles, and we decide to call it a night.

As the six of us stand to head in, Jill speaks up. "Boys, your father and I have been talking, and we've decided you can switch rooms, if you want to, that is."

Nathan and Liam look at each other in surprise.

"Seriously?" Liam asks.

Jill nods. "I know we've been hard on you both, but I didn't want any funny business while Nathan was still young. Then, when you were with Anna, Liam, we wanted to ensure she felt comfortable here. But you all are adults now."

Something has shifted in the family dynamic, and I wonder what Liam thinks of the change.

A smile forms on my face as we head inside.

The alcohol has me feeling reckless, and I want to ride my cowboy 'til the sun comes up.

Anticipation tingles through me as we head up the stairs, Liam's touch on my lower back setting my skin on fire.

We reach the top of the steps, and Riley gives me a playful wink as she and Nathan disappear into the boys' old room.

Liam and I reach our room, and he pulls me inside with a swift push of the door. I've been looking forward to this all night, but I didn't think we'd get a chance to do anything until we got back home.

Liam keeps the lights off and sits on the edge of the bed. Moonlight streams through the window, reflecting off the water in the distance.

He crosses one leg over the other and grips his boot, but I place a gentle hand on his wrist to stop him. I don't know what entices me to do this, but I drop to my knees in front of him, easing his boot off.

His face remains neutral, unreadable. I swallow hard before I decide to keep going and remove the other boot. I toss it to the side and look up at him.

He grips my throat, lifting my face towards him so he can touch my lips with his. The taste of his tongue intoxicates me as I run my hands up his thighs, searching for his zipper.

He gently moves my head back, checking in with me, confirming there is no hesitation in my eyes. I don't give him any, and he lifts me from my knees, laying me down on the bed and covering my body with his own.

His lips find mine again, kissing me with unrestrained passion. The whiskey and cigar smell on his breath combined with his masculine cologne turns me on, the sheer essence of him getting my panties wet.

We break apart from the kiss just long enough to catch our breath, Liam's eyes dark with desire.

"You are unbelievably beautiful," he murmurs, brushing a strand of hair from my face.

His lips trail kisses down my neck, and I swear there's no better feeling than his soft lips contrasting with the roughness of his beard.

I tilt my head back as he kisses my collarbone and travels down to my breasts. His beard scratches my skin gloriously, and I lift up to unzip my dress.

He helps me remove it, tossing it on the ground, his fingers finding my lace underwear and rubbing against my core through the fabric.

"Oh, angel, are you feeling needy?" he says in a husky whisper.

I nod, too horny to speak.

"Are you gonna be quiet?"

I nod again.

"Good girl."

He pushes my panties to the side and rubs two fingers through my slit, coating them in my wetness before circling them around my clit. I moan softly at the sensation.

"Shh," Liam whispers against my neck, and I press my lips together to keep from making any noise.

The calloused pads of his fingers rubbing circles around my clit makes it difficult to focus, and I struggle to stay quiet. I writhe underneath him as he brings me to euphoria.

An old bed squeaks from the next room, and I giggle drunkenly. Liam shakes his head, the rhythm coming from next door leaving no room for doubt about his brother's activities.

"Just ignore it," I whisper.

We continue kissing as he fingers me until Liam can't take the sound anymore. He jumps off the bed and pulls a box fan out of the closet, plugging it in and turning it on high. The fan drowns out the sounds of lovemaking in the next room, and he climbs back on the bed with me.

I turn him over and straddle him, wearing nothing but my lacy underwear. There's something unbelievably hot about being nearly naked on top of him while he's still fully clothed. His fingers find my clit again, and I ride his fingers until I soak them.

The fan has me feeling brave enough to get a little louder, and I let out a quiet cry of pleasure as I come. I take deep breaths and come down from the high as Liam watches me with dark eyes.

Now that my panties are ruined, I hop off the bed and

lower them down to my feet, removing them and tossing them aside. Liam sits up on the edge of the bed, his feet on the floor, and holds his arms out to me.

I wrap my arms around his neck and stand between his legs, completely naked, feeling vulnerable and submissive. I want to worship every inch of this perfect man. My lips grace his neck, kissing and licking the smooth skin.

I cup his beard with both hands and step out to spread my legs around his. He doesn't look away from my eyes as he inserts two fingers inside me, curling and straightening them over and over until I can't take it anymore.

I shove him back on the bed and lower his jeans, tearing at his shirt until he pulls it over his head. I move to climb over him, but he stops me and lowers me to the bed, my head resting on the pillows as he removes his underwear.

He fingers me just enough to ensure I'm wet, and I stare back at him in total bliss. I give him a naughty smile as I take in the sight of his hard cock, subconsciously spreading my legs further for him. He positions himself between my legs, resting back on his knees as his cock rubs against my pelvis. He pushes down on the base of his cock with one hand, slipping inside me seamlessly, as if this is the most natural thing in the world.

He thrusts in and out of me, and I sit up on my elbows to watch his abs contract with the movement. He grips the outside of my thigh and increases his pace, eliciting moans from me that I have no control over.

His large hand moves to my waist as he continues to thrust. Blonde hair at the edges of my vision blocks out the rest of the world, and I focus on Liam's lean body.

He reaches his other hand out to pinch my nipple, roughly

pulling the stimulated tip. My body bounces against his, making my breasts jiggle and drawing Liam's eyes to my chest.

Liam grips my leg again, lifting it for leverage as he pounds into me harder. Cries of pleasure escape my lips, mixing with the sound of his body slapping against mine. His brows furrow with intensity, and he drops my leg to grip the sides of my neck as he relentlessly thrusts in and out.

He leans down to kiss me, his hands still cupping my neck. Then he drops his head to the pillow, out of breath, a look of total euphoria on his face. He rallies and lifts himself up again, bracing his arms on either side of my head. I gingerly touch his toned stomach, loving how his muscles feel as they contract under my fingertips.

He slows his pace, the sound of his balls slapping against me making me feel dirty in the best way. Feeling kinky, I open my mouth, stretching out my tongue. He gets the hint and spits in my mouth. The crude act turns me on, and I giggle playfully.

I open my mouth again and stick my tongue out, looking up at him. He spits in my mouth again, this time leaning down to lick it off my tongue, sucking my lips in a wet kiss.

He keeps his slower pace, and I bite my lip to keep from moaning too loudly. Wanting another sloppy kiss, I purse my lips and wait for him to oblige. He bends his elbows enough to meet my lips, giving me a demanding kiss.

"*Mmm*," he moans against my mouth.

He slows to a stop, breathing deeply to avoid coming. He finds my lips again, kissing me and keeping his hips still. I kiss him back and rub my hands over the muscles of his back.

He moves to pull out of me, but I give him a playful slap on the ass—aka *get going*. He obliges and slowly enters me again, pulling almost completely out before entering each time.

He holds himself up by his arms and quickens his pace again.

I kiss down his side, resting my fingertips gently on his waist.

"*Oh*," he moans in his deep, throaty voice before collapsing on top of me, the flood of his release hot inside me. He rests his forehead on the pillow. "Oh my God," he breathes.

He pulls out and rolls to the side, giving me a full view of his delicious body. Wrapping his hand in my hair, he pulls me to him for a punishing kiss.

I open my eyes to see Liam lying there, beaming—the biggest smile I've ever seen from him. He closes his eyes and falls asleep, still smiling.

Chapter 35
Liam

The sun begins its ascent over the lake, casting rays that paint the water in shades of pink and orange. As usual, I'm the only one up. Mornings like this bring me peace before I have to deal with other people.

Sipping coffee from a mug, I lean back in my chair. My brother inherits this place in five years, so I'm trying to enjoy the lake house before he turns it into party central. I'm sure he'd let me come up for boating weekends, but his friends are... How do I put this? Dumbasses.

I left Sienna sleeping in our bedroom, her hair spread like a halo on the pillow. I'm more than happy that my parents seem to like her so far, but I don't know what today will bring. Sienna couldn't be more different from Anna, and they loved her. My parents' approval means a lot to me, especially my dad's, but even if they don't approve, I would never end things with her.

The sun rises further in the sky, and my dad's footsteps tell me he's up too, walking around inside. The door slides open, and he joins me with his own coffee mug. We sit in silence and enjoy the view until he finally speaks.

"Sienna seems nice," he says, opening the dreaded conversation of my love life.

"She is."

"How'd she like the farm?"

Translation: *Is she a city girl or will she fit in with us?*

"She loved it."

"That's good," he says. "I'm looking forward to getting to know her better."

I don't know how to answer that, so we simply sit there and watch the water until the rest of the family wakes up.

Joining Mom in the kitchen, I mix pancake batter as she lays bacon strips on the griddle. I'm bracing myself for her version of the same conversation, but she just continues laying bacon down.

Once she's done, she turns to me. "Today should be fun. We missed you last time."

I nod and hand her the bowl, and she takes it from me to start the pancakes. The last time they came up to the lake house, I was too depressed to get out of bed. With just a few messages from Sienna later that night, I was meeting her the next day for a date.

As Mom pours the pancakes onto the griddle, she's smiling more than usual for a typical boat day.

"What?" I ask.

She shrugs. "You seem happy."

"I am."

She's smiling like a goofball, so I decide to go find Sienna instead of continuing whatever *that* conversation was.

I head upstairs, but Sienna isn't in our room. I close the bedroom door and look around the hallway to find her brushing her teeth at the bathroom sink. When she sees me, she lets the toothbrush dangle from her mouth and gives me the come-here signal with her finger.

I join her in the bathroom and close the door. She turns back to face the sink, bending over to spit out the toothpaste. She replaces her toothbrush in the holder and wipes the corners of her mouth as she looks at me in the mirror. I wrap my arms around her waist and kiss her neck, eliciting a quiet moan from her.

"We don't have much time," I whisper in her ear, sliding my hand down her flat stomach and into the band of her shorts. I watch her eyes in the mirror as I rub the outside of her underwear. Dragging my finger up and down her panties, wetness coats my finger.

She reaches behind my head and threads her fingers through my hair. The desire in her eyes makes me want to yank her shorts down and enter her from behind, but there's no time.

"Are you wet for me, angel?"

"Yes," she breathes.

I pull my hand away and back off, smirking.

She turns to face me, her jaw dropped in disbelief. "You're not gonna finish what you started?"

"There's no time."

She smirks and places her hands on my hips, gently shoving me against the door. She lowers her body down, pressing her tits against me all the while until she's on her knees, massaging my balls through my sweatpants. I groan as she grips my cock through the fabric and smiles up at me seductively. The sight of her on her knees in front of me has my shaft rising to attention, and her seductive smile turns into a smirk again.

She rises slowly, placing her hands against my chest.

Leaning in, she whispers in my ear, "Have fun being hard at breakfast."

Sienna and I sit curled up in the back of the boat, my arm draped over her shoulders. Her golden hair is twisted into a braid, and her tits press together in a bright blue bikini. The color draws out the tan of her skin, and her toned body makes her the envy of every woman on this lake.

Dad parks the boat at the marina, and he and I run in for supplies. When we return, a teenage dock hand is chatting up Sienna.

"I know my way around boats. I could help you out with all kinds of stuff," he says, leaning cockily against a post. "Anything you need, really."

Sienna, focused on rubbing sunscreen on her arms, barely acknowledges the kid.

"Thanks," she mutters.

"I could help you with your sunscreen if you want—"

"I got it. Thanks," I say sternly.

He glances at me before scurrying off to assist another boat. Rolling my eyes, I hop back into the boat and slide into the driver's seat. Sienna smiles, squeezing sunscreen into my waiting hand. She turns so I can get her back, and I know I'm acting like a smug bastard as the guys on the dock watch me rub sunscreen all over her smooth skin.

I anticipated this, that all the guys would be drawn to her. It doesn't bother me. My girl works hard on her body, and I don't give a fuck if she shows it off.

Once we're sunscreened up and untied from the dock, I turn my hat backward and start the boat. Sienna watches my every move from the passenger seat as I back up and steer the boat into open water. Her impressed expression feeds my ego. I didn't think I could get any more smug, yet here we are.

The wind in my hair invigorates me, though not quite as much as the angel sitting a few feet to my left. I speed up, curious to see her reaction. Sienna's smile widens, clearly having the time of her life out on the open water with me and my family. I crank up Dad's classic rock station, noticing Nathan and Riley watching me from the front.

I navigate through the crowded cove, turning it down as we tie up next to some family friends.

"Liam! Is this the new girlfriend we've been hearing about?" Mom's friend Liz asks.

Sienna beams. "Yes, that's me. I'm Sienna."

"Well, aren't you a pretty little thing," Liz gushes. "Nice job, Liam!"

I don't react, but inside, I'm grinning like a kid on Christmas morning. Sienna is mine, and I want everyone to know it.

My girl crosses over to the other boat with my mom and gets introduced to everyone. She sits in between two people she just met, and she already has them laughing. Riley heads over to join the women, and I settle in next to Nathan in the front of the boat.

He gives me a knowing look, but I don't bite. I wait for him to talk, but he still doesn't say anything; he just gives me that look. The boat rocks us gently, and eventually I cave.

"What?"

"You *liiike* her," he singsongs, dragging the word out like we're ten years old.

"She's my girlfriend," I say matter-of-factly.

"I know," he says before walking to the cooler and grabbing two beers.

As he sits back down, I reach my hand out for one.

"I'm double-fisting today."

I roll my eyes and head to the cooler to get my own beer.

Halfway through our beers, Nathan gets serious. "I can tell it's different with her. You were never like this with Anna."

I hate talking about relationships and feelings, but my curiosity is piqued. "What do you mean?"

"You're way more affectionate. You tease each other. She makes you smile."

I would've thought he'd tease me about being all lovey-dovey with Sienna, but he's actually serious.

"I'm glad you're getting back out there. I hope she sticks around."

I nod slowly. "Me too."

We finish our beers and grab a couple more, soaking up the sun and listening to music like we always do on boat days.

We both glance over at the same time to see our girlfriends lying on their stomachs on the back of the neighboring boat and talking behind their hands. They giggle like schoolgirls at something Riley said, and Nathan turns to me.

"Bet they're comparing our dick sizes."

I roll my eyes and walk away, hopping across to the other boat. I find myself wondering if that *is* what they were talking about. I'm not comfortable with others knowing the intimate details of our sex life, so if that's what they're talking about, I want to put a stop to it.

"Do you want something to drink?" I ask Sienna.

"The boat over there has frozen drinks."

I look over to the boat she's talking about. It's a group of college-aged kids, drinking some kind of red slushie drinks out of plastic cups.

"We only have beer and seltzers," I tell her.

"That's okay. I'll just go ask them if I can have some of theirs."

I'm taken aback for a second. "You're gonna swim across the water to a boat full of strangers and ask them to make you a frozen drink?"

"Yeah," she says nonchalantly. She slips gracefully into the water and starts to swim over to them.

Riley stands beside me, and we watch as Sienna reaches the other boat.

"She's a firecracker," she remarks.

"You have no idea," I mutter, recalling the firecracker popsicle from a few weeks ago.

Sienna stays in the water and talks to one of the college guys on the boat. I stand there with my arms crossed as she chats this guy up. Eventually, he walks away and comes back with a cup full of red frozen drink and a straw.

Sienna swims back to our boat, and I help her back up. Her body is absolute perfection as she stands in front of me, dripping wet. The college guys are ogling her, so to shield her from their wandering eyes, I place a possessive hand on her back and guide her back into the boat.

I sit Sienna down on the seat and glare at the guys on the other boat with my arms crossed.

"It's a strawberry daiquiri," she says, taking another sip.

"Stand up," I command.

She rises immediately, and I cup her face and kiss her passionately. Jealousy making me bold, I reach my other hand down and cup her ass cheek, turning her so the college kids can see my hand on her ass.

I pull away from the kiss and look down into her eyes, finding a look I know well. She's turned on. I exhale in relief that I didn't ruin things between us with my need to claim her.

Whoops and cheers erupt from our boat and the one next to us, snapping me back to reality. Sienna and I sit down, and I drape my arm around her.

I feel a little awkward that my family saw me do that, but Sienna seems perfectly content, sipping on her daiquiri.

As the sun sinks towards the horizon, Sienna and I join Nathan and Riley at the front of our boat. They've all had a lot to drink, and I'm probably the most sober one here. Somebody's gotta keep their head and get us home.

"This is awesome!" Sienna gushes, her eyes bright with excitement. "My first time on a boat did not disappoint," she says, slurring just a bit.

Nathan chuckles. "I can't believe you've never been on a boat before."

"I don't know anyone rich enough! My family doesn't have a lake house or a farm or a boat..."

"Well, now you know us," Nathan says.

"I'm glad I do," she replies, looking around at all of us. "Get used to me 'cause I'm gonna be out here with you guys every summer!"

I let those words wash over me like a wave. She likes the idea of a future with me.

"One day we'll have our own boat," I tell her.

"Our own boat?" she says in disbelief. "*And* a farm? I'm so happy you're my boyfriend!" she says, laughing.

Riley gives her a look at that statement, which gets me thinking about what Sienna is actually saying. I know she's a little drunk, so I need to take everything she says with a grain of salt (much like she did with the tequila shot she downed earlier), but sometimes the truth comes out when alcohol is involved.

I decide to let it go, and the conversation ventures into how different our lives were growing up. Sienna didn't go to private school or on vacations like Nathan and I did. She and her brother shared a bedroom growing up; they even shared a car. It's no wonder she's so excited about being on a boat.

"Do you think your dad will let me play music?"

"No," Nathan, Riley, and I say at the same time.

"Let's see!" she says, bouncing over to my dad to ask if she can play some music.

"Sure, sweetheart," he answers, surprising all of us.

I raise an eyebrow and exchange a look with Nathan. A minute later, pop music plays through the speakers. A few people sing and dance along, and even though I detest pop music, I like seeing my girl happy. The change in the atmosphere is evident as people start to sing.

Sienna and Riley join some girls their age in the next boat over, and they start dancing like they're in a club. The next song begins, the dirty lyrics sounding across the five boats tied together, and more people start to get up and dance.

I move to the driver's seat of the boat to get out of the sun and get a better view of my girl. As the third song plays, the lyrics get even dirtier, and all the pretty girls dancing in bikinis

214

start to draw attention from other boats.

Nathan and I watch as the girls grind against each other, but only one of them draws my attention.

She's the sexiest one here, the sexiest on the whole lake if you ask me. She throws her arms in the air and shakes her hips back and forth to the suggestive lyrics, and suddenly I can't wait to get her back home in my bed.

Until she bends forward slightly and shakes her ass against some other girl's butt.

Their bottoms reveal more than they cover, and their bare ass cheeks bounce off of each other, something I should probably find sexy as hell, but I don't. In fact, it pisses me off. My jaw tightens as I watch her, anger and possessiveness building with each passing second.

They're dressed in practically nothing—their bottoms are barely more than a thong—and the filthy lyrics add to the crudeness. I glare over at her, but she doesn't notice. I want to put a stop to it, but I don't want to be the asshole that ruins her fun.

I'm torn, and I look over at Nathan for help. He's leaning back with his arms over the sides of the boat, feet up and beaming smugly. Clearly he sees nothing wrong with the situation. Although it's not his girl that's practically making a porno.

Hell, maybe there isn't anything wrong with what Sienna's doing... I shift my gaze to some of the other women and realize it's only Sienna and that other girl acting like that.

Am I overreacting? Letting my possessive streak get the better of me?

After a few agonizing minutes, the song ends, and the next

song is not quite as filthy. The girls sing loudly and jump up and down to the chorus.

I'm no prude, but there's a line between dancing and having fun and dirty dancing practically naked with a girl you just met. And Sienna crossed it.

She hops back over to our boat and tries to put her arms around me, but I bristle at her touch.

"What's wrong, baby?"

"What was that?" I say, letting my anger come through in my voice.

"We were dancing."

"Yeah, I saw that. I meant with that girl."

"Which one? I was dancing with all of them—"

"The one you were rubbing your bare butt cheeks against." I cross my arms over my chest, noticing that our argument has caught the attention of my family. I lower my voice. "Your swimsuit barely covers anything."

Sienna's eyes flash with anger. "So? I can wear whatever I want. And I can dance however I want—"

"I don't give a f—I don't care if you dance. I'm glad you were having fun. And I like that you show off your body. What I care about is you not dirty dancing with a half-naked girl." I run my hands through my hair in frustration. "I just didn't like it, okay?"

Understanding takes over her face, and she hangs her head in shame. My parents awkwardly avert their gazes, but Nathan and Riley openly stare. I didn't mean to embarrass her, but I had to say how I felt.

"I crossed a line. I'm sorry if I upset you," she says quietly. "I'm not used to thinking about anyone else. I dance like that with my girlfriends all the time, I didn't even think..."

My anger begins to melt. "It's okay. But you can't just do whatever you want anymore."

"I know. I'm sorry. I won't do it again."

I take a deep breath and wrap my arms around her waist, pulling her in. "I can't stay mad at you," I say—for the first time in my life.

Chapter 36
Sienna

Liam forgave me quickly, but the worry that I might have upset him more than he's letting on hangs over me. I got too drunk and danced too obscenely. I embarrassed him—and myself. I didn't touch another drop of alcohol after that.

The sun disappears into the water, plunging the lake into darkness, and we wait on the boat for the fireworks show to begin. It's tradition for the family to watch the show from the water, which is why they packed sweatshirts and blankets.

Liam and I are snuggled under a blanket, my back flush with his chest. The cool breeze off the water soothes my sun-kissed face, and I tilt my face up to the sky to watch the show begin. The gentle rocking of the boat is soothing, and Liam's arms around me and steady heartbeat ground me in the moment.

I meant what I said—I'm not used to thinking about anyone else. My life had been a series of impulsive actions, doing whatever I wanted whenever I wanted. But I can't be reckless anymore. I need to stop and think before I act. I can't lose Liam; he means everything to me. My mind replays the scene from earlier, wishing I could take back my actions.

I turn my head and nuzzle into his neck, whispering, "I'm sorry," needing to know we're okay.

He kisses my forehead, his lips soft and warm. "Shh," he whispers, looking into my eyes. "I told you, it's fine."

Fireworks reflect in his eyes, and tears form in mine. "I let you down," I choke out.

"No, you didn't, angel. I overreacted," he says softly. The fireworks boom loud enough that no one can hear us. "You were just having fun." His hands rub up and down my arms, calming my thoughts.

"A little too much fun," I say, defeated. "You had every right to be mad at me. That was unacceptable." I'm overcome with emotion, the stray effects of the alcohol probably.

He gives me a soft smile, brushing a stray hair out of my face. "Just don't let anyone touch you but me. You're mine, and I don't share." His attempt at humor lightens the moment, and the lump in my throat finally disappears.

I smile up at him, watching the fireworks show through the reflection in his eyes. He doesn't look away either, and we gaze at one another, communicating silently how much we care for each other. His intensity doesn't unnerve me like it used to. Now I find it reassuring.

My heart swells with uninhibited love for him. We haven't said the word out loud yet, but I know Liam feels it, too. I see it in the way he looks at me, the way he holds me, the way he forgives me.

I rest my head on his chest again, wondering why I'm so sentimental about everything tonight. I recall all the times Liam made me smile. Playing in the backyard with Zoe, falling asleep next to each other, the necklace he gave me. Each memory in my mind shows the love growing between us, a love that feels more real with each passing day.

The fireworks burst above us, each explosion lighting up the night sky. I smile to myself, knowing I'll remember this summer forever.

The summer we fell in love.

After a long day on the water, we finally get back to the lake house. Liam's parents head straight to bed, but the four of us grab some beers and head out to the fire pit. The crisp night air offers a refreshing change from the earlier heat, and the stars are scattered across the sky like diamonds, reflecting off the lake's gentle waves.

We sit in a semi-circle around the fire, facing the water and talking about the new change in sleeping arrangements. The fire crackles in front of us, sending up occasional sparks.

"I still can't believe it," Nathan says, shaking his head. "It must've been Mom's idea. Dad's too stubborn to change his mind."

"I mean, it's pretty obvious why your mom would be on board with the idea," Riley says.

Nathan and I look at her in confusion.

"Because she's ready for grandbabies."

Riley laughs as Nathan almost chokes on his beer.

"Jeez, I hope it's not that," he coughs. "More likely it's because Anna isn't around anymore."

Riley shrugs. "Yeah, you're probably right."

"Do you know about that?" Nathan asks, looking my way.

"Yeah, Liam told me," I answer. "She didn't sleep in the same bed as him."

"Fucking weird, right?"

"I don't think it's weird," I say. "I can understand her

220

wanting to wait until marriage."

Nathan gives me a look. "Well, I always thought it was weird. I thought a lot of things about her were weird."

"Yeah, like how she never posted on social media," Riley chimes in. "She didn't want her picture on the internet at all."

"That's smart of her," I defend. "There are some creeps out there."

"Yeah, but come on. She wouldn't even let *us* post a picture if she was in it," Riley says. "And the way she dressed..." She grimaces. "She would wear floor-length skirts with cardigans over God-awful blouses. I've actually seen her wear an honest-to-God pearl necklace. I've never seen anyone under the age of fifty wear one."

My anger rises, and I take a deep breath, giving myself a moment to think before I speak. "There's nothing wrong with being modest," I say simply, taking in the warmth of the fire.

"Yeah, I guess," Riley concedes. "I just remember *begging* her to let me give her a makeover, and she always said no."

"That was a lost cause, babe," Nathan tells Riley. "It would've taken a miracle."

I glance at Liam to gauge how he feels about the turn of conversation, but he simply stares at the fire, holding a beer in one hand.

"No offense, bro," Nathan adds, glancing at Liam, "but she wasn't much to look at—"

"Okay, that's enough. You don't have to be a jerk," I snap at Nathan. So much for thinking before I speak. My voice carries a sharp edge, and a twinge of guilt tugs at me for speaking to Liam's brother that way.

Nathan holds up his hands in apology. "You're right, you're

right. I'm just saying she was very plain. You're a total upgrade."

"That's not a compliment," I retort. I take a deep breath to calm down. "I just don't like being compared to other women. And Anna must have been pretty great if Liam loved her."

Nathan simply nods. "He did love her. I just don't understand why," he says with a chuckle.

I cross my arms, and Liam watches me out of the corner of his eye. I wonder if he's surprised that I came to his ex-girlfriend's defense.

I lean over to him. "I wouldn't want them to talk about me like that if we ever..."

He reaches out to squeeze my thigh, speaking in a low voice that only I can hear. "The fact that you can't even finish that sentence makes me lo—" His eyes widen as he stops himself, letting the unfinished confession hang.

I can't hide my smile as I lean in to kiss him. I want to say it too, but now's not the right time. Besides, we both know we're in it for the long haul.

"So, Sienna," Nathan begins, changing the topic. "How do you like the farm?"

"It's beautiful," I say dreamily. "I live in a studio apartment right now, which always felt small, but it feels microscopic now that I've seen the farm. Aren't you jealous that your brother gets to inherit all that land?"

"Nah, he can have it. I get this place. Lakefront property, boats, jet skis. I got the better end of the deal."

Liam speaks up for the first time tonight. "You do realize the boat and jet skis don't come with the place? Those are still Mom and Dad's."

Nathan frowns. "Damn, I didn't think about that. Well,

I'm sure they'll leave them here, so I can use them anytime I want. They'll basically be mine."

"Well, *I'm* jealous," I continue wistfully. "I'd love to live on that much land. I've always wanted to have a butterfly garden where I can just sit and watch them flutter around and a field of wildflowers I can walk through. Ooh, and a flower garden with fairy lights and a picnic area where I can host a book club or something. It would be so magical." I say, getting excited about all the prospects.

I glance at Liam out of the corner of my eye, but he's on his phone, texting someone.

Nathan beams at me as if he knows something I don't while Riley sits in her chair, stone-faced.

"Do you make enough money for that?" Riley asks.

Shit. Here we go again. I thought Riley had gotten over her skepticism of my intentions with Liam, but apparently not.

"No, definitely not," I say with a chuckle, trying to de-escalate. "It's just a dream right now. Maybe one day."

"I see," she says, still sounding unconvinced. "Liam, can you help me get my suitcase? I left it in your guys' room last night."

The two of them head inside, leaving me alone with Nathan.

We sit in awkward silence, staring at the flames. The night suddenly feels cooler, and I put my hands in the front pocket of my sweatshirt.

"I'm sorry I called you a jerk," I say after a while. "I get defensive when men start judging women's choices."

"No, I was a dick," he admits. "That all came from a place of resentment. I saw what she did to my brother."

"She made a choice. A stupid one, for sure," I joke. "But I'm glad things didn't work out with her."

He nods slowly. "You're much better for him. You bring him out of his shell, get him to do things he'd normally never do."

I smile at his approval before he pins me with a serious look. "Please don't break his heart."

"I don't plan to," I assure him.

"Good. Should we head in?"

I nod, ready to curl up next to Liam in our bed. It's been a good day overall, but it's also been intense, and I'm desperate to be close to him and share some quiet time together.

I stand as Nathan puts out the fire the way men do, and I leave him to do his business.

Inside the house, I head for the stairs, but Riley's voice stops me in my tracks.

"You heard what she was saying. She wants to get out of her apartment, but she's stuck. I'm gonna put this plainly: you are her one-way ticket out."

I stop in the middle of the stairs, my heart thumping in panic as I wait for Liam's reply.

"I think I mean more to her than a piece of land."

"Six weeks isn't long enough to know that. Does she know how much money you make?"

"What's that supposed to mean?" he asks, anger lacing his tone.

"I think you know exactly what it means. I just find it a little suspicious that this random woman reached out to you out of nowhere. She's beautiful and sexy and fun and..."

"And?"

She takes a deep breath. "Look, you're a great guy, but a girl like that doesn't just instantly fall in love with someone," she says gently. "She's charming you to get what she wants," she says, as if she doesn't want to be the one to tell him.

"Then why did she want me to return the five-hundred-dollar necklace I bought her, huh?" he snaps.

Five hundred dollars? I feel the blood drain from my face as my fingers find the diamond around my neck.

Riley doesn't have an answer.

"I'll tell you why. Because she said she doesn't want expensive stuff. She just wants to spend time with me. Does that sound like a woman who only cares about money to you?"

"I hate to say this, but that could just be part of the act. If she knows you make hella money, then of course she'd try to convince you she doesn't care about that."

I expect Liam to defend me again, but he stays quiet. My heart breaks with each second he remains silent.

"Look, I don't know how to explain it, but my woman's intuition is telling me something is off here. Just be careful," she says pointedly. "Don't do something you regret forever."

"Why don't you just say exactly what you mean?" Liam says bitterly.

"Be *careful*. I won't let her trap you into marriage."

Her harsh words cut deep, and tears spill from my eyes.

"You have no idea what you're talking about," Liam says harshly. "Why don't you mind your own *fucking* business and worry about your own boyfriend."

I cover my mouth with my hand. He broke his no-cussing-at-a-lady gentleman's rule. I silently run down the steps, crashing into Nathan's chest at the bottom.

I bounce off him and look into his chestnut brown eyes, an identical match to his brother's.

"I don't believe any of that," he tells me earnestly.

I try to wipe away my tears, but they just keep coming. "Thank you."

Nathan gives me a comforting smile. "Riley means well. She's just very protective of the people she loves. She'll come around," he assures me.

All I can do is nod. I appreciate his words, but Riley's accusations cut right through my heart. "Can't blame her for that. I would do the same for my brother."

We head back to the fire pit, and I help Nathan gather the empty beers and put out the fire properly. The night is quiet, the earlier tension slowly dissipating as we work in silence. Once everything is cleaned up, we walk back into the house together.

We turn out the lights before heading upstairs. I have a sick feeling in my stomach at the thought of Liam finding out how I found him, and I decide then and there to never tell him the truth. Riley's intuition is sharper than most, and I'm impressed she listened to it and took action to try to protect Liam. If I can convince her I'm not a gold-digging baby-making harlot, I think we'd be pretty good friends.

Upstairs, I hesitate outside our bedroom door, then take a deep breath and push it open. Liam looks up from the bed where he leans against the headboard.

"Hey," he says softly.

I climb into bed next to him, and he puts his arm around my shoulder, kissing my temple.

"You didn't have to defend Anna like that, you know."

"I couldn't stand hearing them talk about her like that. No one deserves to be judged for their choices, especially when they don't know the whole story."

"I love your big heart," he murmurs, his voice warm with genuine affection.

His words erase some of the tension I've been feeling all night.

We sit quietly for a while before I speak again. "I care about you. More than I can put into words." I want to tell him I'm not with him for his money or his land, but I don't want him to suspect that I overheard his conversation with Riley.

"I care about you too," he replies, his eyes meeting mine with sincerity.

The events of the night fade away in the sanctuary of our room, and despite everything, I feel at peace. He's with me, ready to face whatever comes our way.

I lift my head to kiss him, and neither of us feel like stopping. We kiss until his body covers mine, and we remove our clothes seamlessly. We're completely in sync as we roll around on the bed, the passion between us undeniable.

He lays me down and enters me smoothly, wrapping his arms around my back and holding me close. This time, the sex is sensual, meaningful. He locks eyes with me, then quickly turns away. It's a fleeting moment of vulnerability, and I can't help but wonder what's going through his head.

I kiss his neck as he gently thrusts in and out, my hands pressing against his back. The physical connection feels incredible, but our emotional connection feels off.

He breathes deeply, his orgasm building. At the last second, he takes a breath in and pulls out completely, resting his cock on my stomach. Hot spurts paint my belly as he comes down from his release, his body trembling.

I lie still until he rolls off of me and covers his face with his hands.

"Liam?" I say softly.

He shakes his head back and forth, turning his body away from me, leaving me lying there, alone.

He doesn't completely trust me yet.

The realization stings, and something in our relationship shifts.

I fight tears as he stands up and puts his pajamas on before going out into the hallway. He returns with a small towel and wipes my stomach clean, his touch gentle but distant. Neither of us know what to say, so we get ready for bed in silence.

When I eventually fall asleep, it's to the sight of Liam's back, his body turned away from me.

Chapter 37
Liam

Our forks clink against china bowls in the silence of my house. Sienna sits across from me in a cropped white top and black loose-fitting shorts, diamond necklace resting on her collarbone.

Things have been tense since we got back from the lake, like we're just going through the motions. We've been spending time together at either her place or mine every day, but the underlying tension remains. We have a lot to talk about, but for some reason, I can't bring up any important topics. It's as if there's an invisible barrier keeping us from getting to the heart of the matter.

I hate to say it, but Riley's warning got to me, and it's driving a wedge between me and Sienna. Riley made a lot of good points. This woman I don't know randomly reached out to me and got me to fall for her, hard. Sienna is unbelievably beautiful and fun. Why would a girl like that want to be with me when she could date a professional athlete or a male model? Doubt and fear gnaw at me, making it hard to focus on anything else.

"This is really good," she tells me, breaking the silence. "You have a gift."

"Thanks," I mutter. A pang of guilt hits me for not being open and honest, but I continue the small talk. "I know your stomach turns into a black hole when you're around pasta, so I made sure to make extra."

"And I appreciate that," she teases, scooping more pasta into her bowl.

Her smile seems forced, like she can sense the change. Who am I kidding? Of course she knows. She's not stupid.

We eat in silence until I can't take it anymore. "Are you on birth control?" I blurt out, the question escaping my lips before I can stop it.

Her eyes widen in surprise at the sudden topic change. "Yes, of course I am," she tells me, as if she can't believe I'd ask that.

I breathe a sigh of relief, and she clinches her jaw at that. "I just wanted to make sure."

Her brows furrow slightly as she stabs at her tortellini, the motion almost aggressive. But I'm sure I'm imagining that.

"If we ever did, you know, have an... accident, I'm not going anywhere. But still, I'd rather not make any mistakes—"

"Liam," she interrupts, frustration evident in her voice. "I can't believe you think I would have unprotected sex with someone I've only known for two months. Do you really think I'm that careless?"

"I just wanted to make sure."

She puts her fork down harder than necessary. "Well, you can breathe easy. I have an IUD. Do you believe me, or do you need proof?"

"What's that supposed to mean?"

"You've made it very clear that you don't trust me."

Her pointed look tells me she's noticed that I've been pulling out the past few times we had sex. The realization that she's aware of my actions hits me in the gut.

"Can you blame me?" I avoid her gaze and continue eating, even though my appetite is gone.

She stands and takes her bowl to the sink. The clink of the ceramic echoes loudly in the silence.

I regret my words instantly, and I sit there, wondering how I can fix this. My doubts and insecurities press down on me more and more with every passing second.

"I've never given you any reason not to trust me," she argues, the hitch in her voice betraying her upset. "I would *never* put you in a situation like that."

"But how do I know that?" I turn to face her in my chair. "You don't seem to care about anything. You do whatever you want whenever you want and damn the consequences."

She crosses her arms over her chest and glares at me. "Is this about dancing with that girl on the boat? I thought we moved on from that."

"It's... everything. You're so self-assured that nothing bothers you. A woman from work calls herself my work wife and you don't care. You make less than minimum wage working for your friend's gym—you don't care. So excuse me for assuming that you would be careless about something like birth control."

"That's completely different! Just because I'm self-confident doesn't mean I would risk putting you in a position like that."

I bring the dishes to the sink, and she steps out of my way as I rinse them and put them in the dishwasher. The tension is almost suffocating. We might as well get it all out now.

I turn to face her, leaning against the counter. "You don't have a car. You're stuck in a studio apartment. You don't have any plans for your future. There's a difference between being carefree and being irresponsible."

"I can take care of myself," she says sternly, her eyes blazing with determination and anger.

"I really don't think that's true." My words hang in the air, and the hurt on her face makes me want to take them back.

Tears form in her eyes. "Where is this coming from?"

I tear my gaze away from her watery hazel eyes and glance out the back door. "I need to be cautious."

"So I don't ruin your life," she says bitterly. Tears fall freely down her face. "I shouldn't have even come here tonight. I blew off a fun night with my friends, again, because you didn't want to go."

"Yeah, I don't want to hang out with your friends. They're shallow, and all they do is gossip."

"I love my friends. I can't keep blowing them off because you don't want to hang out with them."

"You'd rather spend time with them than me? Sienna, they're not good friends. They've caused you nothing but heartache the entire time I've known you."

"Well, they're still my friends. Through good times and bad."

Her loyalty to them softens my heart, and I close my eyes. Isn't that exactly what I've been searching for? Someone who's loyal no matter what?

"You can hang out with your friends if you want. I'm not stopping you."

"I want you to go to the fair *with* me," she says, her voice breaking. "Part of having a girlfriend is doing stuff she wants to do."

"And part of having a boyfriend is respecting his wishes."

"That's all I've ever done," she argues. "I've been the perfect girlfriend."

"A perfect girlfriend wouldn't rely on her boyfriend to drive her all over the state and demand that he go to the fair with her friends when he said he doesn't want to."

"And a perfect boyfriend wouldn't accuse his girlfriend of trying to trap him into marriage! He wouldn't call her irresponsible and insult her friends."

I stand in the kitchen and let the silence stretch. "I'm not your chauffeur," I say slowly. "I'm not your ATM. And I'm not your ticket out of your apartment."

The hurt on her face is too much to bear. "If you honestly believe that that's how I see you, then you can leave me the hell alone."

She heads for the front door.

"So you're really ditching me for your friends?" I shout after her.

She turns around in the foyer. "I'm not gonna sit here and take this."

The door slams after her, the sound echoing through the house, leaving a deafening silence in its wake.

Chapter 38
Sienna

Tears streak down my face as I lift my phone to my ear. "V? Can you pick me up? I'm at Liam's, and we got into a huge fight."

"Oh sweetie, of course! Just text me the address."

I sit on the curb as I wait for her, wiping my tears. Riley's accusations must have gotten through to him. I'd suspected that might be the reason for his distance over the last few days, but I didn't expect him to outright accuse me of dating him for his money.

I thought we were building a solid relationship. We've been vulnerable with each other, opened up about personal things, and spent every day this summer together. Along the way, we developed feelings for each other. Or at least, I did.

Maybe if I'd been more open about my feelings for him, he would trust me. Maybe he wouldn't have taken Riley's warning and we would have gone back to how things were.

Just when I'm ready to rush back inside and tell him just how much he means to me, a black SUV pulls up. V smiles as she rolls down the passenger window. She looks absolutely tiny in the oversized vehicle, and I hop into the front seat.

She pulls away from the curb, and I wipe my tears enough to finally notice she's in her skimpy work uniform.

"Were you at work?" I ask, my voice shaky from crying.

"Yeah, I'm on my break."

"You didn't have to do this. I could've called someone else."

"It's no problem," she assures me. "Am I dropping you off at your apartment?"

"Actually, can you take me to the fair? I need to let loose and hang with my girls."

"Absolutely. I have to head back to finish my shift, but I'll come join you all in a couple of hours."

We ride in silence until we merge onto the highway.

"Do you want to talk about it?" she asks, her voice laced with concern.

I let out a sigh. "I started it. Well, sort of." I don't know how much I can tell her. Liam wouldn't appreciate me disclosing that he's been pulling out when we have sex. He's a very private person, especially when it comes to our sex life.

"He's been different ever since we got back from the lake last weekend. His brother's girlfriend thinks I'm only with him for his money, and I guess that got into his head. I overheard her warning him that I might trap him into marriage, and I can tell he's been suspicious of me ever since."

"Oof, that's rough."

I stare out the windshield, my throat tight with the promise of tears. "I don't know how to get him to trust me," I say, feeling defeated.

"He'll come around, I'm sure. You two are meant to be together."

V's unwavering optimism always lifts my spirits, even when I'm feeling my worst. She's always been a romantic.

I shake my head and smile weakly. "What makes you say that?"

"Because you're crazy about him! And if he has a single

brain cell, he's crazy about you too."

I laugh for the first time all night. "I hope you're right."

She pulls into the parking lot of the fair, and I hop out. "Thanks for the ride. I owe you one."

"Have fun! See you later."

I close the car door, and she waves as she drives off. I turn toward the bustling fairgrounds and head to the ticket booth. Once I have my wristband on, I look around for Amber and Chloe, but it's too crowded to see past everyone.

If I know my friends, they're probably on the dance floor. I head that way, but the band hasn't started yet. I stop at a concession stand and get a cinnamon churro before I continue wandering around the fair.

As I eat the last bite, I spot the two of them out of the corner of my eye, and I chase after them. They head into a building, and I follow after, just a few feet behind. The noise of the fair fades as I step inside, and the harsh fluorescent lights hurt my eyes.

"Can you believe she blew us off again?" I hear Chloe say around the corner. "She's such a hypocrite, choosing her man over her girls."

I'm about to turn the corner, but Amber's voice stops me.

"She brags about him so much, I'm glad she stayed home."

I stay where I am, listening to their conversation from the hallway.

"Have you noticed that she always makes things about her? It's so exhausting," Chloe says.

"Yeah, and if she stays with Liam, you just know she's gonna brag about how much land she has and how they have a boat and how much money he makes," Amber adds, mocking my voice.

Tears form in my eyes for the second time tonight.

"I know! She's already started with her stupid diamond necklace. It's like she forgot where she came from."

Amber's next words cut like glass. "She likes to act like she's independent, but she relies on Liam for everything. He paid for all our drinks the other night despite looking miserable as hell. Every weekend, he drives all the way to her apartment, then all the way to his farm, then all the way back to her apartment to drop her off before going home again. I bet she's trying to convince him to just let her move in so she doesn't have to pay for rent anymore."

"She probably doesn't even like him. She just likes the attention. She's always preaching about honesty and integrity, but I just know she's faking it with this guy."

"I don't know about that. She does seem to really like him."

"Then I feel sorry for him," Chloe replies. "Her arrogance knows no bounds. She thinks she's a goddess come down to earth to bless us with her presence."

"Yeah, I'm tired of her acting like she's above us. She needs to come back down to earth."

"Exactly! She's just as messed up as the rest of us, yet she has the nerve to criticize us. She's the biggest hypocrite I know."

"Yeah, like her life is figured out! She's—"

I finally step out from around the corner, my cheeks hot with shame and anger. Amber's eyes widen comically, and her mouth drops open.

"Oh, don't stop now. What were you gonna say?" I challenge Amber, who stands there like a deer in headlights.

Chloe cuts in. "We're just telling it how it is. You've always acted like you were better than us," she says with a glare. "You were the best cheerleader on the squad, valedictorian, all the guys wanted you."

Amber stays quiet, looking back and forth from Chloe to me.

"I never thought I was better than you guys. I loved you," I say genuinely. Tears threaten to fall, but I fight them. "You were my best friends. How long have you been talking shit behind my back? Since high school? Middle school?"

"Oh, whatever," Chloe snaps. "You're so quick to point out other people's flaws, but you can't see any of your own."

"I never claimed to be perfect." I shake my head, looking at Amber, who hangs her head in shame. "You know, I might have expected this from Chloe, but I thought you'd at least have my back. We've been friends since kindergarten."

Amber has always given in to peer pressure, and I know she only went along with Chloe to feel included. Chloe's been putting thoughts into her head for years, making her hate me. That explains why she's been acting out the past few weeks. I'm pissed at Chloe, but I'm disappointed in Amber that she would throw our friendship away.

I look away and take a deep breath. "Does V talk about me too?"

Amber shakes her head. "No."

I breathe a sigh of relief. At least I have one friend left. "I'm guessing you talk shit about her too?"

They don't bother defending themselves.

"I'll let her know. Don't expect me to be in touch because I won't. I never want to talk to you two again."

I turn to walk away, but I can't resist. I turn back around. "By the way, Chloe made out with your boyfriend Kyle in ninth grade."

"You bitch!" I hear as I walk away.

I throw the building door open and storm out.

Part of me wishes I'd never come tonight, but mostly I'm just glad I found out the truth. God, Liam was right. He saw through our years of friendship and realized how they really felt.

I head toward the fair's exit, fuming. I risked my relationship to come here, and they treated me like dog shit under their shoes—and they have been for the majority of our so-called 'friendship.' I should've known. They'd often tried to gossip about other girls to me, but I'd always put a stop to it. Of course they would just continue when I wasn't in the room.

Taking out my phone, I set the GPS to guide me home. It's a long walk, but I know V's in the middle of her shift, and I can't call Liam right now. Everything is falling apart, and I don't know how to put my life back together.

After three miles, my feet start to ache, and my chest feels tight with every step, but I push on, driven by anger and sadness.

Eventually, after six long miles, I reach my apartment building. I trudge up the stairs, ready to make myself a stiff drink to drown my sorrows. But when I reach the top, I spot a familiar tall and lean figure leaning against my apartment door.

"Liam!" I run to him.

He wraps me in his arms, and I bury my head in his chest as tears stream down my face. Sobbing, I let him hold me as I fall apart.

"I'm so sorry," I mumble into his chest, my voice muffled.

He gently rubs my back. "Shh, it's okay," he murmurs. "I'm sorry, too."

I pull back slightly to look up at him, my eyes red and puffy. "I don't care about your money, Liam. I care about you. I thought you knew that."

He wipes a tear from my cheek with his thumb, his eyes filled with regret. "I do know that. Of course I do. I just let my doubts get the better of me. I'm sorry I hurt you, angel."

We head inside, and Liam makes us both a warm drink while I change into comfier clothes.

Sitting on the couch, I tell Liam what happened at the fair, about Amber and Chloe's betrayal. "You were right. I can't believe I didn't see it before."

"I'm so sorry, Sienna. You don't deserve that."

I nod, a fresh wave of tears threatening to spill. He pulls me close, kissing the top of my head. The weight of my friends' cruelty slowly lifts from my shoulders as he holds me.

"Will you stay here with me tonight?" I ask.

"Of course," he says, wrapping the blanket tighter around my shoulders.

I rest my head against his chest and let my thoughts wander. The pain of losing my friends is still fresh, but tonight gave me a sense of clarity, too. This is my chance to start over, to surround myself with people who genuinely care about me.

"Thank you," I whisper, my voice hoarse. "For being here. For believing in us."

"Always."

"You and me."

"You and me," he echoes.

As we sit there, wrapped in each other's arms, I feel a glimmer of hope. Despite the betrayal of my friends, I know I have someone who loves me for who I am.

Chapter 39
Liam

Saturday morning brings soft sunlight and Sienna sleeping next to me. It's early, so she probably won't be up for a while. I take the time to watch her sleep. She lies on her stomach with her head turned towards me, her hands under the pillow.

I brush a strand of hair away from her face to reveal her delicate features. Her soft skin and peaceful expression make my heart swell. She breathes deeply and quietly, completely at peace. Seeing her like this fills me with an indescribable sense of contentment, like this is all I'll ever need.

I want to adore her and care for her in every way possible. She deserves to be appreciated.

I run a finger up and down her spine, careful not to wake her. I know now that I'm going to love her forever. From our weakest moments to our strongest. When she's sad, when she's happy, and everything in between. I want her to be unapologetically herself, and I will prove that I'm worthy of her with my actions, not simply my words.

I run my finger up and down her back, tracing patterns, and she breathes deeply in her sleep. My mind drifts to the first time we met, how she drew me in and made everything else fade away.

I resign myself to the fact that I'm totally in love with her. And it was easy to fall in love with her, not because she's beautiful and confident and fun, but because it was what I was meant to do. I love her so intensely that it feels like my entire being is burning. It's exhilarating yet comforting at the same time.

She's it for me. I feel it in the depths of my soul. My life changed for the better after I met her, and it will never be the same. I stare at her sleeping form, saying the words in my head. *I love you.* The thought is so strong, it feels like the words leap from my chest and wrap around her.

She slowly opens her eyes, gazing into mine.

Her knowing look has me curious, but before I can say anything, she whispers, "I love you too."

At first, I think she read my mind, until I realize I must have been tracing the words on her back. A smile forms on her face, and she lifts her head to kiss me. I wrap my arms around her and pull her in, smiling against her hair.

"I love you," I tell her out loud this time. I messed up last night. I let my fear and doubt get the better of me, and I want to fix that today. "And I'm so sorry about last night. I didn't mean anything I said. I don't know what came over me."

"I'm sorry too," she whispers, nuzzling into my neck. "If my headache and cramps today are any indication, I'm the reason we got into a fight."

I don't hesitate to jump up and head to the medicine cabinet in her bathroom, returning with a bottle of pain reliever and a glass of water. She smiles as she sits up to take them from me, swallowing two pills.

I leave the room to give her privacy and sit at the kitchen table. My past girlfriends, especially Anna, never talked about their periods with me. I mean, I knew it happened, but I never knew when, so I'm not quite sure what to do. I want to comfort her, but I'm not sure how.

I could get breakfast ready. I can't go wrong there, right? She usually starts her day with that God-awful gritty 'coffee' shake, but I can do better than that. I heat up some oil on the stove and make her protein drink while it heats up.

Sienna comes out of her room in a comfy blue sweatshirt and sweatpants and hugs me from behind. "What are you making?"

"Homemade donuts," I tell her. "The way my grandma showed me."

"Aww, that's so sweet," she teases, coming around to kiss me. "You're the best." She takes the protein drink I made her with a quick thank you and sits at the kitchen table. I know her well enough now to know that her lightheartedness is just a front. She's still upset about what happened with her friends.

As I shape donuts out of raw biscuits, I notice her staring out the back window. I want to give her a hug, but I shouldn't leave the stove. This apartment is tiny, so I need to keep an eye on the hot oil.

Still, I have to say something. Even when her friends were inconsiderate or downright rude to her, she was always doting on them. They've been friends since sixth grade, and they had a lot of fun memories together. I know the loss of them is cutting deeper than she's letting on.

"Do you want to talk about it?"

She shrugs. "That part of my life is over." Her watery eyes stare down at the table.

I drop the donuts one by one into the hot oil. "I guess you're not going to talk to them anymore?"

"I already blocked their numbers." She smiles sadly and shakes her head. "I should be glad they were only talking about me and that they didn't chop off all my hair in my sleep." She plays with her necklace. "The worst part about hearing them talk about me like that was that I had to pay forty bucks to hear it. Now I'm broke for the rest of the week."

I use tongs to remove the donuts from the oil and drop them into a bowl of cinnamon sugar. I wish I could just hand her forty bucks to make her feel better, but that feels like crossing a line. It's hard not to be able to solve all her problems, but I know sometimes you have to just listen.

Setting the plate of donuts on the table, I sit across from her.

"At least I got a churro out of it," she says, picking up a donut and taking a bite. "Mm, this is so good. How are you such a good cook?"

I shrug. "I used to cook with my mom as a kid."

We eat in silence as the sun rises and brightens the apartment. Sienna brushes sugar off of her hands and heads to the coffee maker. She brews me a cup, adds just a little bit of sugar, and sets it in front of me, kissing me on the cheek.

I happily take a sip. "I should be the one doing stuff for you," I tell her as she sits back down.

She gives me a soft smile. "I'm feeling fine. I'm moving on to bigger and better things."

"Happy to hear that." Her emotional resilience is astounding. She's proven that time and again. How her ex-boyfriend treated her, our fight, her friends talking about her behind her back. I can't help but admire her ability to move past heartache and see the bright side of things.

We finish breakfast and clean up, settling into an easy domesticity.

"I had an idea for that, actually," I tell her as I'm washing up.

She gives me a confused look.

"Bigger and better things," I explain. "A way for you to make more money."

"Well then, I'm all ears."

"If you're comfortable with it, you could film your Pilates classes at home and sell them as a package online. Or you could make a couple of videos a month and have people subscribe to your channel. It'd be a way to make passive income and reach a bigger audience."

She seems to think about it before nodding enthusiastically. "I like that." She leans against the kitchen counter. "But I have no idea how to do that kind of stuff. I'd have to market myself."

"I could help you."

A huge smile forms on her face. "Let's do it!"

Sienna bounces on her heels, her eyes sparkling with excitement.

"I love how excited you get. It's kind of adorable," I blurt out, the words slipping from my mouth before I can stop them.

I'm not usually so candid with compliments, but with Sienna, it feels natural.

"You're telling me I could work less often but make more money," she marvels. "How could I not be excited?" She takes both my hands in hers. "With your smarts and computer skills on my side, I'll be making money in no time."

She looks at me like I'm capable of anything, and her confidence in me melts away my insecurities. I look away to hide my smile.

"You smiled! I saw it," she exclaims, beaming. "There's no denying it."

"Not everyone can smile all the time," I mumble, trying to deflect the attention. "Except maybe you."

"Well, I better take a mental picture to savor it."

I roll my eyes. "Stop looking at me like that."

"I can't help it. You're so cute!" she says, peppering kisses over my cheeks and jaw.

My face gets hot at the attention and compliments she's giving me. I've never been good at receiving affection, but with Sienna, I'm learning to love it.

She finally pulls back. "So, what do we do first?"

"Are you sure you're up for this?" I ask, worried about both her physical and mental state. "Filming the videos?"

She tilts her head. "I am pretty bloated," she jokes. "And I don't even know where to film. I don't have much space here."

We return to the small kitchen table, our knees touching. The closeness feels intimate, grounding. "How would you feel about filming the videos outside? We could find some scenic places for nice backgrounds."

"Yes! I love it," she says, her eyes lighting up with the idea. "I'll get started planning the workouts."

She darts to her room and returns with notebooks and pens.

"I'll need my computer at home to build you a website, but we can get started here," I say, already mentally mapping out the website's layout and design.

We dive into logistics and create a plan. She writes everything down in the notebook, from her experience and credentials to a short bio for her website. As she jots down workout routines, I visualize how to translate her vibrant personality into a digital space.

Her energy is infectious, and I find myself getting excited as well. If we can get her started making solid passive income, she can quit working at so many gyms. Plus she'll have more time to spend with me.

"Maybe we could take a little road trip, find ourselves some locations," I suggest, half-joking, half-serious. Taking a trip together somewhere that isn't one of my family's properties feels like taking the next step in our relationship.

"That's a great idea! Just you and me, exploring and working together."

I nod, feeling a surge of determination. "Let's do it. I have some vacation days I can use. We can take a long weekend."

"I need a weekend like that," she sighs, a dreamy look in her eyes.

We continue planning her online presence and the trip. As the hours pass, my excitement builds, not just for our trip but for Sienna's future. This is her chance to move up in the world. She's got the energy and drive, and I've got the technical know-how. Together, we can create something remarkable.

I have no doubt she's got the talent to succeed. This is her world. I'm just grateful to be a part of it.

Chapter 40
Liam

The following Friday morning, Sienna is waiting in the parking lot by her apartment, clutching two packed bags and a yoga mat. She hops into my truck, buzzing with energy, and as I pull out of the spot, a smile finds its way onto my face.

As we cruise down the highway, heading towards the first state park on our list, Sienna's leg bounces, her gaze fixed straight ahead. I thought she was just excited, but her usual relaxed and confident posture seems tense.

"How are you feeling about this?" I ask, glancing over at her. She's dressed in a matching teal sports bra and leggings.

"I'm kinda nervous," she admits.

"Don't worry. Even if you mess up, we can always edit the video later."

"You're right." She takes a deep breath, flipping down the visor to check her makeup.

"I'm hoping I've found some good spots, but I've got backups if those don't work. I figured you could film two videos at each spot. That'll give you enough content to get started."

She looks at me with genuine appreciation, her eyes softening. "You didn't have to do all that." Moving to the middle seat, she places her hand on my leg. "You're the best."

A little while later, we arrive at the first location—a gravel parking lot that leads to a hidden gem. We hop out and follow the trail that winds through the trees until it opens up to a breathtaking waterfall cascading into a creek. The real-life view far surpasses any picture I saw online, and the roar of the water adds to the serene ambiance.

Sienna spreads her oversized yoga mat on the lush grass, beginning her stretches as I set up the tripod on a fallen log. We spend a few moments perfecting the angle, ensuring the waterfall frames the backdrop before I hit record. Sienna, in her teal workout outfit, blonde hair pulled up into a messy bun, looks like she belongs on the cover of a fitness magazine.

I stand behind the camera, captivated as she flows through a Pilates routine for beginners with effortless grace. It's my first time seeing her in action, and she's even more mesmerizing than I imagined. The rush of the waterfall is too loud to hear anything, but we plan to add the voice-over later anyway.

She finishes her routine and bounces over to me, her excitement evident.

"Let's watch it back!"

We sit on the log, reviewing the footage. It turned out great.

"Oh my gosh, I look so professional!" she says, her hazel eyes sparkling. "Okay, let's film the next one."

I marvel at her ambition as she takes to the mat again. She waits for me to give her the thumbs-up before she begins the next workout routine.

Once we're finished at the waterfall, we drive to the next spot—a vibrant field of wildflowers. She films two more videos there, her energy unwavering. By the time we reach our final location for the day, it's mid-afternoon. Sienna films the last two videos in front of a majestic rock formation, pushing through her fatigue.

As the day winds down, I can see the exhaustion in her eyes, so we stop at a restaurant. She slumps into the booth across from me, clearly drained. Not only has she recorded six workout videos, but we've also had to hike quite a bit to get to some of the spots.

"It'll all be worth it," I assure her.

"I know it will," she replies with a tired smile.

"I've been working on your website after work. It's all done. We just need to upload your content."

"Thank you so much. I really appreciate this."

Our food arrives—steak and shrimp for me, a grilled chicken salad for her.

She catches my puzzled look and explains, "I don't want to look all bloated for the camera."

I simply nod, respecting her choice, but inside I'm concerned. It doesn't seem like enough calories for what she's accomplished today.

After dinner, I take us to our hotel for the night. The lobby is adorned with sparkling chandeliers and velvet couches. Sienna's eyes widen with amazement at the grandeur, taking in every detail with childlike wonder.

We ride the elevator to the top floor, its mirrored walls and gold accents adding to the sense of luxury. I'm sure this hotel is a step up from what she's used to, and her sense of wonder is adorable as we step into a hallway lined with plush carpeting and elegant artwork.

I take her hand and lead us down the hallway, using the key card to open the door. Stepping inside the spacious room, Sienna takes it all in. The king-sized bed dominates the space, but her gaze shifts to the hot tub, then to the balcony with its stunning view of the forest.

"This place is incredible!" she says, running to the balcony. "I could sit out here all night." She stares at the scenery for a moment before shaking her head. "I need to hop in the shower first." She comes back over to me and lifts up on her toes to whisper in my ear, "Meet me in the hot tub."

Her words send a thrill through me as she disappears into the bathroom. Anticipation builds as I start the bubbles and get the water hot. Once I'm naked, I step in and lower myself down, the bubbles gently massaging my skin. Sienna emerges from the bathroom a few minutes later, stark naked.

She saunters over to me seductively, and I thank my lucky stars that she reached out to me two months ago. She steps into the hot tub and lowers herself across my lap, cupping my face as she kisses me.

I tilt my head back as she trails kisses down my jaw and neck, reaching my hand down to tease her clit. She spreads her legs wider and lets out a moan against my neck.

"I want you so bad," she murmurs. She lifts her head to kiss me. "I've been thinking about this all day." She trails her tongue up my neck and to my ear. "You make me so wet," she whispers, her dirty talk making my cock hard.

Linking her fingers with mine, she shifts my hand so she can rub her core against my cock, her other hand behind my neck. "I love how hard you get for me."

Her filthy mouth turns me on and ignites a fire inside me. "Do you want to fill me up, baby?"

I can only nod as she lifts herself up and lowers her body down, impaling herself on my cock.

"Just like that," she gasps.

I circle her nipple with my tongue, eliciting even louder moans from her.

"That feels so good."

Her words of praise stroke my ego with the same intensity as her pussy stroking my cock. Her bare tits bounce in front of my face, and the pleasure builds to an unbearable level.

I gently press two fingers against her clit as she rides me, her movements becoming faster and more urgent. She leans down to kiss me, increasing the pace.

"*Ah*, I'm going to come," she gasps.

We both reach our climax together, our mouths meeting as I release my cum inside her. Our heavy breaths fill the steamy air as we relax into the hot, bubbling water. She slowly lifts herself off my lap, water dripping down her glistening body as she moves to nestle into my side. I wrap my arm around her waist and plant a soft kiss on her forehead.

"I am so proud of you," I whisper.

"For riding your dick like a pro?" she teases.

"That, and everything else you accomplished today."

She smiles up at me, the reflection of the dim lights sparkling in her eyes. "I couldn't have done it without you."

I carry Sienna's suitcases up the stairs to her apartment after a long drive back. Exhausted, we collapse onto her bed. We had gotten into a routine over the past few days: traveling to state parks, hiking to scenic spots for her videos, and retreating to the hotel to unwind. We fell into the rhythm naturally, the two of us working together seamlessly.

We have twenty videos to go through and edit, then she'll record the voice-overs. But for now, we're finally relaxing. Holding her in my arms, I gently thread my fingers through her hair.

"You didn't have to do all this, you know," she murmurs, her voice soft.

"I wanted to."

"Well, I appreciate it. Especially the massages you booked for me. That was a nice touch—literally."

"I figured you'd be sore."

"You really thought of everything. I'm impressed."

"I'm the one who should be impressed. You made enough content this weekend to tide you over for the next six months at least."

She kicks her feet in excitement. "What do we do now?"

"You never stop, do you?" I tease.

She shakes her head. "Not really."

"Do you want to see your website?"

"Umm, *yes!*" She leaps out of bed and grabs her laptop, returning to sit beside me. We lean back against the headboard as I pull up her website. Her jaw drops at the sight of the landing page.

"That actually looks professional!" she exclaims in disbelief.

I give her an offended look. "I'm a software engineer. What did you expect?"

"I know, but... Liam, this is amazing!"

I shake my head, amused, and guide her through the different pages. "Here's where we'll advertise the different packages, and here's where people can learn more about you.

We just need to upload the videos."

I transfer the videos from my phone and show her how to edit them. We work on two of them, and she records the voice-over instructions. As we wait for them to upload to the website, I explain that these two will be free samples to help get people hooked and give them more incentive to buy the packages.

"This is so cool. I could actually make money doing this," she says as if the realization is just now dawning on her.

"As long as you market yourself. First, we need to look at your online presence. Do you have any embarrassing or unprofessional videos or posts?"

She thinks for a moment. "I don't think so."

"Let's check." I type her name into the search engine and scroll through the results. Finding her LinkedIn page, I click on it and hand over her laptop.

She updates her bio and picture, adding the link to her new website. She hands it back to me, and I review the page.

"I think you need something more catchy. A strong headline will make or break you. Here, let me show you mine."

I open up a new tab, type my name plus 'LinkedIn', and hit go. The search results come up instantly, and I notice that the link to my page is purple—she's looked me up before.

A strange feeling washes over me, and I can't move. Something tugs at the back of my mind, but I can't figure out why. I click on the page, and she reads my bio over my shoulder.

I swallow hard. "Would you mind grabbing me a glass of water?"

"Sure."

Once she's gone, I open her search history, scrolling down

until I see something that stops me in my tracks.

'Software+engineer+salary'.

Angry heat floods through me as I look at the date: May 28. The day she messaged me. Based on the time, she searched this not long before reaching out to me.

My heart sinks into my stomach. That's why she reached out. That's why she came on so strong at the cafe. She molded herself into my perfect girl so that I would be entranced. And I was, like an idiot.

She steps back into the room with a glass of water, but I can't look at her. I stand and turn the laptop to face her, and her eyes go wide.

"Liam—"

"Don't." I shove the laptop towards her and head for the door.

"Liam, wait, please."

I shove my boots on, avoiding her gaze.

"It's not like that."

"Was it before or after, Sienna?" I know the answer. I just want her to admit it.

She stands there, looking like her world is falling apart in front of her. "Let me explain—"

I'm out the door before she has a chance.

Chapter 41
Sienna

He left.

I still can't believe it. No 'how could you' or 'I trusted you'. No raised voices, angry footsteps, or slamming doors.

He just walked out.

My heart plummets as I bury my head in my hands, hot tears streaming down my cheeks. The weight of regret presses down on my chest, suffocating me. I ruined everything. The love of my life walked out the door, and I was powerless to stop him. My chest tightens, every breath a painful reminder of what I've done.

Collapsing onto the cold floor, I hug my knees tightly to my chest. He's gone. His absence is like a black hole, sucking all the warmth and light from the room.

He has every right to be furious. Not only did I search his salary before messaging him, but I also kept it a secret from him. I had so many opportunities to explain, but I couldn't bring myself to. I can't help but replay all our moments together in my mind, each one now marred by the knowledge of my deceit.

I think back to that day in his truck when he opened up to me about his intentions when we first met. The memory stings, and I pound my fist against the floor. Why didn't I tell him then? The words had been on the tip of my tongue, but fear held them back.

I didn't think he'd ever find out. But that's no excuse. He was always honest with me while I've been hiding this secret from the beginning. My deception fills the apartment like a thick fog, suffocating and relentless.

Tears stream down my cheeks as I rise to pour myself a drink—straight whiskey in a glass. The fiery liquid scorches its way down, mirroring the anguish in my chest. I deserve much worse for what I've done. I betrayed him. After all he did for me, all the love and support.

Liam—sweet, caring Liam—is too good for me. I don't deserve him. The thought of his rare but gentle smile, his comforting presence, and his unwavering support intensifies the ache in my heart.

Tears continue to fall as I pour another glass. The room spins slightly, but I don't care—anything to numb the pain.

I glance around my apartment, filled with bittersweet memories of us. The book on the coffee table he read to me, the picture of us on the wall taken on the boat, the couch where we spent countless evenings wrapped in each other's arms. Every detail reminds me of him.

Sinking back onto the floor, I clutch the bottle and the glass tightly. The amber liquid sloshes over my hand and onto my clothes, adding to the mess that my life is now. I feel like I'm drowning, and it's my own mistakes that are pulling me under.

If only I could rewind time, to that moment in the truck, and tell him the truth. But it's too late now. The damage is done.

I wake on the cold kitchen floor, the early morning sun creeping through the back window. The hardness beneath me makes my head throb with every beat of my heart.

I struggle to lift myself up off the floor. I grip the counter, but my vision swims. I close my eyes, cursing the half bottle of whiskey I drank last night. It's not sexy when I do it.

Sudden nausea seizes me, and I scramble to the bathroom, barely making it to the toilet before I vomit. Definitely not sexy.

What have I done? My fingers rake through my tangled hair, and I heave into the toilet again. With each retch, I tell myself I deserve this.

Slumped on the bathroom floor, feeling utterly pathetic and ashamed of myself, I picture the betrayal on Liam's face when I walked back into the room yesterday. I have no doubt he's as heartbroken as I am.

Because of me.

His ex may have shattered his heart in the past, but I tore it right from his chest.

I wipe my mouth with the back of my hand and push myself up to the mirror. Yesterday's smudged makeup and tangled hair stare back at me, and I shake my head in disgust. Stripping out of my clothes, I step into the shower and let the hot water scald my skin.

My muscles ache from all the hiking and making videos, but I barely notice. Everything we built together is crumbling down, and it's no one's fault but my own.

I have to fix this.

After quickly washing my body and hair, I step out of the

shower and wrap myself in a towel. How do I even begin to make things right with Liam?

Feeling desperate, I reach for my phone to call him, but deep down, I know he probably won't answer.

Feeling defeated and miserable, I collapse onto my bed and let the tears flow freely. I allow myself to be pathetic for a while until I have to force myself up to head in to work.

The day drags on with Pilates classes and laps around the track until I finally arrive back home. I've texted and called Liam ten times, but he won't answer.

Evenings blur together in a haze of ignored text messages and editing workout videos. I can't muster the energy to do the peppy and encouraging voice-overs. Not when my heart is breaking.

By Friday morning, I know I have to explain myself to Liam in person, so I wait until lunchtime, grab two Philly cheesesteaks, and stand outside Riley's law firm, waiting for my link to Liam to walk by.

Riley steps out of the building at precisely 12:15. She startles for a moment when she sees me but quickly recovers.

"I know you probably don't want to talk to me right now, but—"

"Why wouldn't I want to talk to you?" she asks, confused. "Come on in."

She gestures for me to follow her before I have time to question her reaction. Did Liam not tell his family about our breakup? Or maybe... we didn't really break up after all.

We step inside the break room and sit at a quiet table in the corner. I'm hoping no one interrupts us this time.

"I know we don't have a lot of time, so I'm just gonna jump

right in," I say nervously.

She looks back and forth from me to the food.

"Sorry, go ahead," I tell her, holding my hand out to encourage her to dig in.

My food sits in front of me untouched as I explain myself. "I overheard you and Liam talking after the fireworks show."

Guilt flickers across her face. "I'm really sorry about that—"

"You were right," I interrupt her. "I got drunk one night and decided to quit dating apps and try LinkedIn instead to find my own match. That's how I came across Liam's profile, and I was drawn to him. But... I never told him that." Tears form in my eyes. "He found out last weekend because he saw my search history where I looked up how much software engineers make. Now he thinks I only dated him for his money." My voice cracks as I continue my confession. "But that's not true—at all. I love him. I really do." Tears fall as I think about how deeply I've hurt him. "And I don't know what to do because he won't answer my calls."

Riley carefully sets her sandwich down and lets the information sink in. "You broke his trust. You should've just told him the truth."

I nod, wiping my tears. "I know."

She bites her lip thoughtfully. "There might be something I can do."

Chapter 42
Sienna

With the contracts in hand, I pace my living room, trying to figure out how to get to Liam's house. Riley drew up three versions—a prenuptial agreement, a cohabitation agreement, and a relationship agreement—and I've signed them all. Each one outlines financial arrangements, property ownership, and individual assets. Riley walked me through each one, ensuring that I understood every clause and condition. Now all that's left to do is to get these to Liam—and get him back.

The city buses can only take me so far, and I'm too strapped for cash to call an Uber. V works weekends, so I can't ask her to take me. Hitchhiking is too dangerous, and I can't walk twenty-five miles to his house. I slump onto my couch in defeat.

I spend all day Saturday recording voice-overs for my workout videos and uploading them to my website like Liam showed me. I take extra care with each recording, thinking of his encouragement, support, and patience with me. If I can make one or two sales, I might have enough money to Uber to his house.

I spend Saturday evening promoting my Pilates packages on various social media platforms, praying for enough sales to make this happen.

Every notification on my phone feels like a lifeline, but

no sales have come through. I monitor the likes, shares, and comments, but so far no one has purchased a package.

As I lie in bed, memories of Liam's support flood my thoughts—his steady hands setting up the camera, the website he created for me, his unwavering belief in me.

I fall asleep hopeful, if not desperate, clinging to the possibility of seeing him again.

When I wake up on Sunday, the first thing I do is check my bank account. To my relief and surprise, I made three sales. Liam would be so proud. A rush of relief and determination surges through me. I jump up to get dressed, choosing the white sundress I know he likes.

After booking a ride, I wait outside nervously, my heart racing. Hopefully these contracts will be enough to prove to Liam that I don't care about his money. It breaks my heart to make our relationship seem so cold and calculated, but if that's what it takes for him to believe me, then so be it.

Ten minutes later, my ride arrives, and I settle into the backseat of the car with the contracts in a folder in my backpack. I rehearse in my head what I'll say to Liam when I finally see him, how I'll explain everything, how I'll make him understand.

As we near Liam's house, my heart races, only to sink when we pull up to his driveway, and I realize that his truck isn't there. He must be at the farm. My hope dwindles, but I refuse to give up.

"Can you take me a few more miles south of here?" I ask my driver, willing him to sense my desperation.

"How many more miles?"

"Eighteen."

"Sorry, that's too far."

I look down dejectedly. It was a risk anyway. I would barely have enough money to get there, and I certainly wouldn't have enough to make it back home again.

But going back home isn't an option either. I'd spend the rest of my money and be back at square one.

"I understand. Thank you." I step out of the car and watch him drive away.

It's okay. I'll just wait here for him. I sit on the front steps, and soon enough, I hear barking from the backyard.

"Zoe? Is that you?" I call out, my heart lifting at the familiar sound.

She barks louder and whines, so I make my way around to the side of the house. We're separated by a fence, but as soon as she catches my scent, she lets out a series of high-pitched cries.

"Hi, Zoe. It's me," I say, trying to get her to calm down.

Our separation only makes her cry harder, so I try to fumble the gate open. It won't budge, and Zoe is barking and crying loud enough to alert the neighbors.

So I do what any sane woman would do. I hop the fence.

My upper body strength comes in handy as I lift myself up and over, dropping down to the other side with a thud. Zoe rushes towards me, her tail wagging furiously as she licks my face and jumps around excitedly.

"Hi, sweet girl," I say, stroking her soft black and white fur. She whimpers and paws at me, her way of saying she missed me. I sit on the grass, letting her affection comfort and ground me.

As I sit in the shade of the fence, I gather my thoughts. I have to make Liam understand that everything we had was real, and I'd be willing to beg on my knees if it meant getting another chance.

I pull the contracts from my backpack and hold them tightly. Whether we're dating, living together, or married, he's not obligated to pay for any of my expenses and his assets are protected.

I can only hope he understands. These contracts are more than just pieces of paper—they're a symbol of my determination to make things right between us.

Chapter 43
Liam

I shouldn't be in here. It just reminds me of what I've lost. The heat of the summer day envelops me as I sit in the shade of the tall trees, their leaves rustling gently in the warm breeze. The air is thick with humidity, carrying the sweet scent of blooming flowers that surround me. The gentle hum of insects and the occasional rustle of leaves do nothing to calm the storm raging inside me.

I should've known. She was too good to be true. Too beautiful. Too sweet. Her musical laughter, her soft touch, the way she looked at me with those trusting eyes—it all felt so real.

But it was fake. Everything. The proof was right in front of me. She knew how much money I made at least an hour before she messaged me. That was all she cared about.

I tilt my head back and gaze up at the sky, the blue expanse offering no answers. I'm never going to move on from this. I know it deep down. A part of me will always be tethered to her. No matter who I date in the future, no one will ever make me as happy as Sienna did. She made me feel alive, as if everything I did mattered. Her betrayal cuts deep. I trusted her more than anyone.

She's the only one who could hurt me this much. She sawed my heart out with a serrated knife, and I left it there, bleeding on her doorstep.

I close my eyes and picture her. It's easy to right now, but eventually I'll forget. Now, though, I remember every detail, every line and curve of her face. My empty chest aches with the memory. I can't even enjoy the peace of the farm. The memories haunt me.

I have to hand it to her. She's a brilliant actress. She had me fooled the entire time, believing that she actually cared about me. God, I should hate her, but I can't find any hate inside me. The only thing I can find is longing. Longing to be with her again, how we used to be, when she would snuggle into me on a lazy morning or surprise me at work.

In the quiet of my mind, I see her. Swinging on the tire swing, her head thrown back in laughter. Touching the necklace as I clasp it behind her. Lying in my arms under the fireworks. How could all of that mean nothing to her?

Every moment we shared plays on a loop in my mind, taunting me.

My eyes fill with unshed tears as butterflies flit about. They go from flower to flower, oblivious to the cruel joke against me. I shake my head and finally leave the small butterfly garden I've built over the past few weeks.

I find myself at the edge of a sprawling sunflower field, the vibrant yellow blooms standing tall and proud under the blazing sun. The sight should bring me some measure of peace, but all I can think about is how Sienna would have loved this place.

The sun starts to dip below the horizon, painting the sky in shades of pink and orange. I wander aimlessly, lost in a maze of memories that lead me back to her every time. I reach the clearing where we laid in the bed of my truck and watched the stars twinkle above.

I imagine her standing beside me, pointing out constellations and talking about her dreams. The silence that used to comfort me now suffocates me with the absence of her laughter.

A shooting star streaks across the night sky, and for a moment, I allow myself to make a wish. A wish for things to go back to the way they were before.

Chapter 44
Liam

As the moon rises in the sky, I begin my journey home. The weekend spent at the farm did nothing to lift my spirits.

I'll have to tell my family that Sienna and I broke up, and she'll become just another ex to them. Riley will say 'I told you so'. Actually, she probably won't. She'll just give me that look of pity. The one that makes me feel like a fool for falling hard and fast and getting burned in return.

How pathetic am I that I want Sienna back? Even if it's all fake, I can't be without her. She can take whatever she wants from me. As long as I have her, I don't care about anything else. The thought of having her in my arms again comforts me. She's like a drug, and I grip the steering wheel tighter as I try to decide what to do.

I shouldn't have left without at least giving her a chance to explain. But as I stood there in her kitchen, I couldn't handle my anger. The pain of betrayal was too raw, too overwhelming. My mind replays the scene, wishing I had stayed, had listened, had fought for us.

Finally, I arrive home, and as I climb the front steps, a voice coming from my backyard stops me.

"... so I guess I have you to thank."

I walk silently around the side of the house.

"I was too nervous to talk to him, but then I saw a picture

of you, and I thought, 'Oh my goodness, I have to meet her.'"

I close my eyes in relief that she's here. The sound of her voice soothes some of the ache in my chest.

"Yes, I did," she baby-talks. "You have a good owner. He pretends to be big and bad, but deep down he's a sweetheart. You love him, don't you? Yeah?" She laughs, her voice catching. "I love him too."

I unlock the gate and push it open, and Sienna turns to look at me, surprise lighting up her face.

"You're home."

Her eyes sparkle as she stands there in the dark, the sight of her making my heart skip a beat.

I nod slowly, my gaze locked on hers. "How long have you been here?"

She shrugs. "A while."

We stand in the silence, tension and unspoken words thick between us.

"Look, I—"

"I shouldn't have—"

We talk at the same time, reminding me of our first date. The memory brings a faint smile to my lips despite everything.

I gesture for her to go first.

She takes a deep breath. "I found you on LinkedIn, not Instagram," she admits. "But it was your picture that caught my attention, not your job title. And I must confess, I may have been a little buzzed at the time. I just remember being drawn to you." She steps closer, and her voice softens. "I was tired of dating apps and meaningless connections, and I just wanted to find someone real. And then I found you. And I'm so glad I did because..." Her eyes begin to water. "I love you.

I'm so sorry I didn't tell you all this sooner."

Tears brim in her eyes, and the sincerity in her voice tugs at my heart.

She pulls a folder out of her backpack on the ground. "Here, these are contracts Riley drew up."

I take the papers from her.

"Whether we're dating or living together or married, you won't owe me anything. Ever. Your assets are protected."

I skim the first contract; it's basically a prenup. The gesture is so unexpected that I don't know what to say. The words blur as I read them, and my mind races with what it all means.

She moves closer again, wringing her hands. "I love you for *you*, Liam. This has been the best summer of my life. I don't care if we live in a dumpster, I just—"

But her sentence is cut short as I tear up the contracts in front of her. She looks up at me, fear and confusion mingling in her eyes.

"You didn't have to do this," I tell her. "I would've given you anything you asked for. All you had to do was tell me the truth."

"I will, always, from now on, I promise." Tears fall freely down her face. "Please give me another chance," she pleads.

Her voice carries something I've never heard from her before—desperation.

That right there is proof that this has always been real. That she loves me just as much as I love her. She wouldn't be begging for forgiveness if it wasn't true. She wouldn't swallow her pride for just anyone.

I hold my arms out. "Come here."

She rushes into my embrace, burying her face in my chest as

we cling to each other.

I wrap her in my arms and kiss her forehead. "Do you want me to take you home?"

She pulls back slightly, meeting my gaze. "I am home."

Chapter 45
Sienna

We pull into the driveway at Liam's house after Labor Day weekend at the lake, and he hops out, grabbing our suitcases from the back. We're both exhausted from the long days on the water and nights around the bonfire.

"Your brother is going to destroy that place," I joke as we walk into the house. I'm ready to shower off all the sunscreen and lake grime.

"Oh, I know. That's why we've gotta enjoy it while we can."

I close the front door behind us, and Liam drops the suitcases and pulls me into him, pressing me into the door. I gaze up into his brown eyes, innocently batting my eyelashes, feeling that familiar rush of excitement.

"Now where do you think you're going?"

His voice sends shivers down my spine.

"Who, me?" I place my hands over my chest, feigning innocence. "I'm an angel."

"You'll always be my angel." He dips his head so his lips hover over my ear. "But now that we're home, I'm going to fuck you like the brat you are," he whispers.

"You'll have to catch me first." I slip out from underneath his arms and dart into the living room, my laughter ringing through the house.

He catches me around my waist and lifts me up effortlessly,

causing me to giggle uncontrollably as he spins me around.

Over the past few weeks, I've quit my gym jobs and pursued an online presence. My audience has grown to thousands, and every day brings new followers. The empire I'm building from the ground up fills me with a sense of purpose and accomplishment.

I've officially moved out of my apartment and into Liam's house—our house. He goes out of his way to make this place feel like my home as much as it is his.

We plan to move into the farmhouse next spring, but he's already shown me the butterfly garden, the wildflower field, and the shelves for my candles.

His family was surprisingly supportive of us moving in together—yes, even Riley. They don't think we're rushing things at all.

Riley has become one of my closest friends. We tell each other everything. Well, almost everything. There's one secret I'm keeping: she's getting a ring very soon.

I've introduced her to V, and they get along like a house on fire. We're soaking up all our time with V before she starts her role as a travel nurse.

I haven't spoken to Amber and Chloe since the night of the fair. Their betrayal still stings, and the memory of their harsh words occasionally resurfaces, but I've moved on. The new friendships I've built and the love I've found with Liam far outweigh the hurt.

And as for Zoe, she's just happy her two favorite people are together. Her joyful barks and playful antics fill the house with warmth and laughter—*inside* the house.

As Liam and I collapse onto the couch, I look around at

the cozy living room, the space that has become our home. It won't be our home for long, but I've realized that home isn't a place. It's a feeling.

Every day feels like an adventure, and the future stretches before us with endless possibilities. And I know, without a doubt, that we'll face it together, hand in hand.

Epilogue
Sienna

"You can do it, angel," Liam encourages me.

I push out a breath. "Don't let go of my hand, okay?"

He squeezes my hand, giving me the courage to push through the discomfort. Sweat beads on my forehead as I focus, the intensity building with each passing second.

"Just a little more," he urges. "There's no turning back now."

My face contorts with effort, every muscle straining to keep going. Liam stands by my side, offering words of encouragement. My grip on his hand tightens, the pain almost too much to bear.

Everything around me blurs, but Liam's hand remains an anchor, grounding me. I let out a pained gasp, and with one last burst of energy, I swallow the last hot dog. The crowd goes wild, and I collapse back in relief.

"Ladies and gentlemen, we have a new champion! Fourteen hot dogs in ten minutes!"

The announcer lifts my hand as the audience cheers. I turn to Liam, his eyes shining with pride and amusement.

"You did it," he says, brushing a strand of sweaty hair from my forehead. "You're amazing."

"I couldn't have done it without you," I pant, still catching my breath. The intensity of the moment slowly fades, replaced by an overwhelming sense of accomplishment—and stomach cramps.

The crowd continues to cheer, their applause a roaring wave of support. As I bask in the glory of my victory, I realize that this ridiculous, hilarious moment is one I'll cherish forever. Liam's hand in mine, the shared struggle, the triumph—this is what love feels like.

And it's perfect.